"*As I shut the door behind him, a wave of defeat washed over me. Whatever—if anything—he felt about me, he'd made it perfectly obvious that I was resistible. . . .*

"*I told myself to forget it. To forget the whole afternoon and to forget Chip. He was just someone with whom I happened to work, and our relationship would be strictly business.*

"*But the pain stayed right where it was. I made my way wearily upstairs to work on some Lovey Hart letters, hoping to take my mind off my own problems by plunging myself into the problems of other people.*

"*It was ironic that the only person Lovey Hart couldn't advise was Caroline Wasserman.*"

"Humorous situations, funny dialogue and perceptive first-person narrative." —*Booklist*

"The relationships have a pleasant spontaneity." —*The Horn Book*

". . . written with Conford's usual briskness . . ." —*School Library Journal*

Dear Lovey Hart, I Am Desperate

A novel by

Ellen Conford

Vagabond Books

SCHOLASTIC BOOK SERVICES
New York Toronto London Auckland Sydney Tokyo

ISBN 0-590-32357-1

Text copyright © 1975 by Ellen Conford. This edition is published by Scholastic Book Services, a division of Scholastic Inc., by arrangement with Little, Brown and Company.

12 11 10 9 8 7 6 5 4 3 2   2 3 4 5 6/8

Printed in the U. S. A.   06

To David and Michael

ONE

For almost a year I was the best-kept secret at Lincoln High. That is, my identity was—or actually, the identity of *Lovey Hart,* who, in reality—

But I'm getting ahead of myself, which is why this sounds so confusing.

The whole thing started one bright fall afternoon in the office (such as it was) of the school paper, the *Lincoln Log.* The first staff meeting of the year had just broken up and I was gathering my books together to leave. Along with the afternoon sun, the sounds of football practice filtered through the windows, meaning that my friend Marty, a second- or third-string quarterback or cornerback (I'm never sure which), was not going to be able to drive me home.

"Carrie, wait a minute. I have to ask you something important."

I

Chip Custer, the editor of the *Log*, walked toward me, his face solemn. We were now alone in the room, and for one wild moment, I thought he might be preparing to ask me something . . . personal. But I dismissed the idea almost before it took shape in my mind. Chip, a junior, who didn't "bother with girls" — according to then-current rumors — was certainly not about to be bowled over by Carrie Wasserman, Freshman Reporter.

"Listen," he began, pulling over a chair, "I had an idea, and I think you'd be just the person to pull it off."

"Uh-oh," I said warily. "That sounds like you've just plotted the perfect bank robbery."

"Not quite," he grinned. He turned the chair around backward and sat astride it, his arms leaning against the back.

"I've been fooling around with the idea of an advice to the lovelorn column, and I think you'd do a great job with it."

"Advice? To the lovelorn? *Me?*" Since Chip never paid much attention to girls socially, I had to assume that he had no way of knowing that I was not exactly Lincoln High's resident sex goddess.

"No, listen," he explained, "I know you're a freshman and it's not like I expect you have the experience to deal with the *really* heavy stuff — "

"Oh, thanks a lot," I said. And stop reading my mind, I added silently. My experience — or lack of it — is none of your business.

"It's just that I think you'd have the right touch for this sort of thing. Those sample columns you wrote when you tried out for the paper showed real potential. What I'd want is light, lively stuff, you know, bringing out the 'funny side of human foibles.' Of course, you could throw in a couple of serious ones too, if you think you can handle them."

If I thought I could handle them! Who spent hours on the phone, listening to the problems Terry and Claudia brought me to solve? Who had the milk of human kindness flowing through her veins where most people kept their corpuscles? Whose shoulder was constantly damp from being cried on?

"Well, of course I can handle it!" I said indignantly.

"Great!" Chip cried, clapping me on my temporarily dry shoulder. "I knew you could. Now listen, the first thing is, this has to be kept absolutely secret."

"What does?" I asked, confused. "The column?"

"No, no, the fact that you're Lovey Hart."

"I'm *who*?"

"Lovey Hart. That's the name we're going to use for the column. 'Dear Lovey Hart.' Isn't that a great name?"

"Chip," I said gently, "that's not exactly one of your top ten names."

"Are you kidding? It's a terrific name."

"Chip, it's corny."

"Well, naturally. It's *supposed* to be corny.

3

Carrie, where's your sense of humor? The thing is mostly in fun anyway."

"Oh well," I said, "if it's *supposed* to be corny, it's a perfectly fine name."

"I knew you'd think so," he beamed.

"What are we going to do for letters?" I asked suddenly. "I mean, the first issue? No one will know about the column — "

"Ah, that's what you think." He whipped a wadded piece of looseleaf paper out of his shirt pocket. He unfolded it and spread it out before me on the desk.

"Posters," he announced. "All over school."

"LET LOVEY HELP!" it read.

"Read 'Lovey Hart' in the *Lincoln Log*! Write to Lovey Hart c/o the *Log* office. Lovey Hart answers your questions, solves your problems, with snappy suggestions for happy solutions!! No names, please — Lovey Hart wants just the facts! Lovey listens — so listen to Lovey!"

"Whew," I said. "Kind of takes your breath away, doesn't it? You don't think it comes on a little too strong?"

"It pays to advertise," Chip declared. "And if this doesn't bring in the letters — we'll make them up ourselves."

"*What?* But that's — "

"Only for the first issue," he hastened to add. "After that we'll have more letters than we know what to do with."

"Well . . ."

"But look," he went on gravely, "this whole

4

thing has got to be kept quiet. You can't tell any-one. And that's for your own protection."

"Good grief, you make it sound as if I'm going to be one step ahead of a lynch mob."

"Well, see, you just don't know. This business of giving advice could get pretty sticky."

I shrugged. I couldn't really understand Chip's supercautious attitude about the whole thing. At the moment, the only problem seemed to be *how* to keep my alter ego under wraps.

"Not even my family?" I asked dubiously.

"Especially not your family!" he groaned. "Caroline, have you forgotten who your father is?"

Ridiculous as that sounds, I had. And I immediately realized that Chip was right — of all the people who mustn't know that I was Lovey Hart, my father was right up there at the head of the list. The head guidance counselor at Lincoln High would probably not look too kindly upon his teenage daughter dispensing solace without a license.

"And besides," Chip was saying, "you lose all the — the — mystery, if people know Lovey Hart is just Caroline Wasserman."

"Oh, yeah," I agreed, with a straight face. "Doesn't have the same ring to it at all."

"You know what I mean," he retorted. "So you make sure no one — even on the staff — sees you pick up those letters. Better yet, I'll hold them for you as they come in. That way — "

"Hey! You're working late!"

5

Chip leaped from his seat, practically knocking the chair over.

"Marty!" I gasped. Chip's leap and my gasp would have planted seeds of suspicion in all but the most innocent of minds. But Marty noticed nothing. I don't mean to malign Marty's mind, because he's a very dear person, and I've loved him like a brother ever since I was in kindergarten and he was in the second grade and he taught me how to print my name. But the fact remains that he noticed nothing, and I realized right away that he *would* notice nothing, being Marty.

"Don't panic," I muttered to Chip. Marty didn't even notice *that*. His long legs brought him from the door to our desks in three strides.

"Thought I'd see if you were still here and needed a ride home," he said.

"Well I am and I do," I replied cheerfully. I stood up and stretched, a little exaggeratedly, as if exhausted by a long afternoon of slaving over a hot typewriter. I was nowhere near a typewriter, but so what?

Chip glanced out the window. The sun was low, and it would be dark in half an hour.

"I didn't realize how late it was. Sorry to keep you so long, Carrie."

"That's okay. Now I have a ride. So long, Chip."

"See you," he said. "Meeting Thursday."

"Need a ride?" offered Marty.

"No, that's okay." Chip waved us out of the room. "I have the car."

Marty drove me home, keeping up a fairly constant stream of chatter about Lincoln's football prospects for this season. I barely listened. Besides being preoccupied with Lovey Hart, I really couldn't work up much interest in football. Oh, I cared enough to want Lincoln to win — I just didn't care to understand all the reasons why it would or wouldn't.

And now, at the beginning of football season, Marty's head was filled with nothing but all those reasons, even though at other times of the year he was a perfectly normal individual who was interesting to talk to. I couldn't blame him, since at the moment my head was so full of my new project I couldn't think of anything else to talk about either. And since I was forbidden, on pain of who knows what, to talk about that, I simply didn't talk at all.

Which was just as well, anyway, since it would have been hard to work a word in edgewise.

"Thanks for the ride, Marty," I said as we pulled into the driveway. "How about coming in for a while?"

"No thanks, it's really late. I'd better get right home."

"Okay; see you."

He drove off and I let myself in the front door.

The odor of something-or-other delicious hit me the instant I walked in.

"Where have you been?" my mother asked, coming out from the kitchen. "Do you know what time it is?"

"Sorry, Mom. We had a *Log* meeting. I didn't realize how late it was. What's that great smell?"

"Garlic bread. Can't you tell?"

"Now that I know what it is I can."

My sister, Jennifer, appeared, apparently from nowhere, and glided past us, a book balanced on her head.

"Hi, Carrie," she said, without moving her lips.

"Hi, Jen. What's that supposed to improve, your posture or your mind?"

My mother grinned. "Really, Jen, you're so old-fashioned. That was something we did back in the old days. I didn't think girls did it anymore."

"I don't know if they do," Jen mumbled, still not daring to open her mouth any wider than a slit, "but I'm doing it."

My mother smiled at me and shrugged. I shrugged back.

"So how was school?" she asked, as I followed her into the kitchen.

"Okay. The same." I practically had to seal my lips like Jen's to keep from blurting out the news. I was dying to tell her. It was really incredible that I — a freshman — had already gotten such an important job on the paper; she'd have been so pleased to know about the column.

But Chip was right. This was my secret, and if

I couldn't keep it the very first day it was entrusted to me, imagine how difficult it would be to keep it later, once Lovey Hart's name was a household word.

Yes, imagine.

TWO

"*I don't like it.*" My father's forehead settled into anxious furrows. "Whoever this Hart is, she certainly isn't qualified to give 'snappy solutions' or 'instant relief' or whatever those posters say."

"Oh, Dad, you're taking the whole thing much too seriously!"

The posters had been up for two weeks, and while they hadn't exactly created a sensation in school, they had stirred up more interest than usual in the paper. And they'd already inspired some letters, which Chip was holding for me.

"And you're not taking it seriously *enough*," my father replied. "The thought of some mixed-up kid giving out advice to other mixed-up kids is absolutely — "

"That's not fair!" I said indignantly. "How do you know she — or *he*," I added quickly, "is a mixed-up kid? Maybe she or he is very sensible."

10

"I'm really tempted," he went on, as if he hadn't even heard me, "to put a stop to the whole thing before it starts."

"Dad! You can't do that. Remember our rule!"

Our rule was that since we were both at the same school, the best way to maintain cordial relations was to never interfere or intrude in the other's sphere of activity.

"This doesn't involve you," he said innocently.

I clamped my lips shut, something I knew I was going to have to get used to doing in the coming weeks but was not used to doing yet, especially with my parents. I hated to lie to them — and I really couldn't remember a time when it had been necessary to lie to them. But this isn't actually *lying*, I told myself. It's just . . . keeping quiet.

"Dad," I said carefully, "I work on the paper, and you want to censor it. That *involves* me. They'd all resent me if you did that. Anyway, you're overreacting. It's mostly for laughs."

"Sometimes things that start out as laughs end up being very unfunny," he said darkly.

"Oh, *Dad*," I sighed.

"Here's one," Chip said, handing me a letter.

We were in the *Log* office, alone, with the door locked.

Chip had had the idea of coming before school instead of staying on after meetings. Since it was very unlikely that anyone would walk in on us at the ungodly hour of 7:45 A.M., no one would ever know we were closeted together.

"Let's see." I took the letter from him.

Dear Lovey Hart:
    I really like this boy, and
most of the time we have no problems, except during lacrosse season.
During lacrosse season, he doesn't
even know I'm alive. All during the
year he's considerate, attentive and
everything you could want. But for
four months out of the year I don't
see him, he hardly ever calls, and
he spends all his time and energy
practicing. What can I do to make
him pay attention to me during
lacrosse season?

                    Yours truly,
                    Anonymous

"Hmm," I said. "A nice problem. Nothing life
or death about that one."

I pondered a moment. Then, inspired, I
scrawled across the bottom of the letter:

Dear Anonymous:
    Everyone has her lacrosse to
bear. Take up tennis and get yourself as involved in that as he is in
his sport. That way, even though he
isn't paying attention to you, you
won't have time to notice.

I went on to the next letter.

Dear Lovey:
    How can I get a boy who sits
in front of me in one of my classes

to notice me? The only time he ever
turns around is when he has to pass
papers back. What can I do to get
him interested in me?

> Sincerely
> B.G.

"Aren't there any letters from boys in there?"
I asked Chip. "This whole column is going to be
how girls can get boys to pay attention to them.
That'll get pretty boring after a while."

"We'll go through the whole bunch of them,
and then you can pick out the ones you like best,"
he said absently.

I sighed, and set my mind to thinking how a
girl could get the right boy to notice her. This, I
thought grimly, is like the blind leading the blind.
If I knew how to get noticed by boys who made
my heart thump and my skin tingle, would I
spend all my time listening to Marty talk about
"red-dogging" or "bull-dogging" or whatever
kind of dog it was that did terrible things to
quarterbacks. (Or was it cornerbacks?)

"Tickle the back of his neck," I wrote, and had
trouble suppressing a silly giggle. Chip looked up
at me; I just smiled mysteriously. "Eventually,"
I continued scribbling, "he'll turn around to see
what's going on. After that, you're on your own."

This isn't bad, I thought, reaching for the next
letter. As a matter of fact, it's kind of fun.

"That's a more serious one," Chip warned. "I
thought we might throw it in for — you know —
tragic relief."

Dear Lovey Hart:

A year ago I was in with a crowd that was involved in the drug scene. It wasn't that I wanted the drugs so much--it was just that these were the only friends I had. So I went along. But I realized I was doing bad things to myself, so after a couple of months I stopped. But now I have no friends, and I'm lonely and all I can think of is that if I get back into drugs I'll have these friends again. At least I'll have someone to talk to, instead of being by myself all the time. I know this is a school paper, so I'm sure you'll tell me to stay straight, but <u>then</u> <u>what</u>? [The words were underlined twice.] I'm getting so tired of being lonely.

Friendless

I slapped the letter down on the desk.

"Tragic relief is right!" I groaned. "I can't answer that!"

"Why not? You have a good head and — I guess — a reasonably good heart. You haven't even tried."

"But Chip, you said this was supposed to be for laughs."

"I said, 'mostly for laughs.' A serious note now and then makes a good column."

I sighed and picked the letter up again. I didn't even know if the writer was a boy or a girl; all I knew was that it was depressing to read, and I couldn't see why a good column had to be assembled out of a mixed bag of hilarity and despair.

Dear Friendless: [I wrote slowly.]
        To have a friend you must
first be one. It's not easy to make
friends, but it's not easy to get
off drugs, either, and you managed
to do that. [I wrote faster now.] Start
by making friends out of acquaint-
ances. Ask one person you like but
don't know very well over to your
house after school. Or to go to the
movies with you. You must take the
first step. Since you've been out of
touch with people for a while, they
don't realize you want to be back in
again.
        Maybe the first person you ask
will reciprocate; maybe not. But
whatever happens, don't stop there.
Ask another person to do something
with you. If you keep on doing this,
soon you will have plenty to do, and
plenty of people to do it with. I
know it's hard, but you owe it to
yourself to try.

        Good luck!

I put down my pencil with a satisfied sigh.

"Not bad," I said. "Hey, Chip, I think this is pretty good."

"Whatever it is," he said vaguely, shuffling through the pile of letters, "don't worry about it too much. Mr. Gross checks all the copy anyway before it's printed up."

Mr. Gross was the *Log*'s faculty adviser. I felt

15

a wave of relief remembering that he'd go over my answers; at least that way, I was sort of off the hook. I mean, if I gave bad advice, he could tell me (or Chip, actually, since even Mr. Gross didn't know who Lovey Hart was) and I could change it. And once he okayed the column, I could be sure I hadn't told anyone anything they shouldn't be told.

I ate lunch with Claudia and Terry, as usual. And as usual, Terry was picking at her food.

"If she gets French right after lunch again next semester," Claudia said grimly, "that girl is going to waste away to nothing."

Terry didn't even look up. Her long hair hid her face like honey-colored curtains as she bent her head. She poked at her tuna fish sandwich with one finger as if she were trying to rouse it from a deep sleep.

"You're denting it, Terry," Claudia warned. "This food is bad enough without dents."

"Oh, leave her alone, Claude," I protested. "It's her sandwich and her appetite!"

"But why does she buy it if she's never going to eat it?" Claudia demanded. Claudia was just slightly plumper than she thought she ought to be, and she tended to overreact when someone else abstained from food without at least a small struggle.

Terry looked up from the sandwich, her dark eyes reproaching us.

16

"Please don't talk about me as if I'm not here," she said softly.

"We didn't know you were," Claudia snapped. "Sorry."

"I can't help it if I'm in love," Terry murmured.

"Oh, for God's sake!" Claudia exploded. She reached over and grabbed Terry's wrist. "Why won't you face the fact that all you've got is a crush on your French teacher? You're no more special than anyone else who ever had a crush — and it's no more love than — than — " Her sputters trailed off in search of the proper comparison.

Terry was unruffled. She looked up at Claudia, blinked her big, sad eyes, and asked calmly, "How would *you* know?"

Claudia flung herself back in her chair and savagely crumpled up the waxed paper from her sandwich. Terry's deceptively gentle question had struck one of Claudia's primary raw nerves — and Terry was perfectly aware of that. She'd been in on the combination soul-search and psychoanalysis session, where we'd tried to figure out why Claudia had never, not once, been in love with anyone. (We ended up with theories — no answers, just theories. The one Claudia liked best was that the boys in school just didn't turn her on. I wasn't convinced that Claudia's problem was all that simple, but it made her feel better to think it was.)

"Why don't you write to Lovey Hart?" Claudia

muttered sarcastically, between bites of her sandwich. "Dear Lovey Hart, I'm in love with my French teacher and he doesn't know I'm alive . . ."

"You'd be surprised — " I began, and nearly dropped my own sandwich. My stomach plunged; I put my sandwich down carefully and tried to keep my hands from shaking.

"Surprised at what?" asked Terry curiously.

I struggled to answer her. I'd been about to say, "You'd be surprised at how many letters start out that way." I couldn't believe how close I'd come to giving myself away, and with hardly any provocation at all.

I mean, no one had backed me into a corner, held a knife at my throat and demanded to know the identity of Lovey Hart.

Maybe that's just it, I warned myself. It's the little slips you have to watch out for. When you expect to be backed into a corner, you have your guard up. It's when you least expect trouble that you're liable to give everything away.

"Surprised at what?" Terry repeated.

"Surprised at Lovey Hart," I managed. "Chip says she — or he — is going to give very sound advice." I *hope*, I added to myself.

"Well." Terry smiled weakly. "Maybe I will write to Lovey."

Oh, don't do that! Please don't do that, I pleaded silently with Terry. I don't want to be responsible.

Chip had come up with the rotten idea of having me answer all the letters we got, whether or not they were used in the column. I pointed out all the flaws in this harebrained scheme, starting out with my own limitations both professional and practical — I mean, I still needed time to go to classes, study, and do other work on the paper, in addition to eating, sleeping, shampooing, and the like — and ending with the impossibility of getting replies back to people who wanted to keep their own identities confidential.

Chip, it seemed, had an answer for every objection. We hadn't resolved the issue yet, but it might be only a matter of time until I had to give Terry sound advice on how to handle a problem I'd been hearing about, but refusing to help her solve, for months.

I didn't have the slightest idea what she should do about her crush on Mr. Stokes. How should I know? The man was unmarried, young and gorgeous. Terry was also unmarried, young and gorgeous. For all I knew, there was no reason why they couldn't run off to Tahiti together and live in a Polynesian paradise for the rest of their lives. Or, for all I knew, there were *thirty-one* reasons why they couldn't.

So when Terry moaned on the telephone to me every other night I listened sympathetically, but didn't offer her anything other than my compassion.

"Who *is* Lovey Hart?" Claudia asked suddenly. "Do you know, Carrie?"

There it was. I've never been a good liar, because I never had enough practice, but here was

19

the corner I'd been afraid of being backed into; there was the knife at my throat, and how could I evade the question?

"It's a deep secret," I said, and took a mouthful of sandwich so I would have something to concentrate on other than Claudia's penetrating eyes.

"No one knows but Chip," I went on. "Not even Mr. Gross knows who it is."

"Well, Lovey Hart herself knows," Claudia said.

"Or himself," I reminded her. Was I overdoing that "she *or* he" bit? It seemed to me I kept harping on it all the time, which might make people suspicious.

"Maybe it's Chip," Terry said.

"Oh, I doubt it," Claudia scoffed. "What he knows about male-female relationships you could write on the head of a pin."

It occurred to me to be glad there wasn't a pin around, otherwise I might be tempted to see if I could fit all *I* knew about male-female relationships on the head of it.

"When does the paper come out?" Claude asked.

"Next Wednesday."

"You know, I never thought I'd look forward to reading the *Log*," Claude said, sounding as if she'd surprised herself. "The only issues I ever saw of it were so dull and rah-rah. Sports and meetings of the Spanish club, et cetera, et . . ."

"Well then, you'll love my articles on the new

cheerleader outfits," I said dryly. "Fits right in the image."

"What in the world," asked Claudia, "can you find to say about new cheerleader outfits, after you've said they're blue and yellow instead of blue, white and yellow?"

"Nothing," I replied. "It's a very short article."

"I guess Chip thought this Lovey Hart column would stir up interest in the paper," Terry said.

"That was the idea," I agreed. "Just to liven things up a bit . . ."

THREE

Dear Lovey Hart,
      I'm in love with my math
tutor. He's a college freshman and
comes to my house once a week to
help me with my geometry. To him,
it's just a business arrangement,
but it's getting awfully hard to
concentrate on geometry when he's
sitting right next to me and
everything.
      What should I do?

                              Nervous

Dear Nervous,
    If you hope to pass geometry,
get a _female_ tutor.

Within a week after Lovey Hart's debut at
Lincoln, the *Log* office was drowning in letters.
Letters arrived via a mailbox stuck up outside the

office, or they were shoved under the door, sometimes so many of them that we had trouble pushing the door open.

There was no question that Lovey Hart was a smashing success. Freshmen who had never scanned so much as a comic book read Lovey Hart. Sophomores, numb from last year's articles describing innovations in the Speech program or the Wednesday afternoon meeting of the Mathletes, or — to be painfully honest — the new cheerleaders' outfits, guzzled Lovey Hart as if they were alcoholics at a wine tasting.

And after they read Lovey, they wrote to her. The first couple of days the letters trickled in. Then the trickle turned to a stream, the stream turned into a river, and the river turned into a deluge.

At the next staff meeting of the *Log*, Chip brought all the letters with him in a shopping bag and heaped them on his desk. It made a very graphic display.

"I think the success of this experiment," Chip declared, "proves to us that the students will read the paper if it gives them what they want."

"I don't think it proves that at all," argued Jessie Krause, Girls' Sports editor. "It just proves they read the new column."

"Yeah, but they actually unfolded the paper this month," said Bob Teal, Boys' Sports. "That's a step in the right direction."

"Exactly," Chip agreed. "At least we've finally

23

gotten them to look at *something* in the *Log*. Now what we have to do is give them more of what they want."

"More Lovey Hart?" I squeaked, cowed by the pile of letters Chip was going to turn over to me.

"No," he said. "Lovey Hart's biggest appeal is to freshmen and sophomores. I want more features, more columns, more humor and human interest stuff — stuff that'll get even the seniors reading the *Log*."

"Why don't you quit while you're ahead?" Bob said. "The seniors have had three years to learn the habit of *not* reading the *Log*."

Cindy Wren, who wrote the Student of the Month column, nodded. "Yeah. If you've got the freshmen and the sophs reading us, that's five hundred more readers than we usually have."

"What I want from you people is ideas," Chip went on, as if Cindy and Bob hadn't even spoken. "I want you all to come in next Tuesday with a special interest feature — a column, a story, something other than straight news. And Cindy, no more twirlers and Honor Society members, for God's sake. Find us someone no one knows, who's doing something *really* unusual."

"Tell me who Lovey Hart is," Cindy retorted, "and I'll write you an interesting column."

"Never mind," Chip said. "Just get me someone different for a change."

The meeting broke up into work sessions. Jessie went out to get a story about field hockey; Cindy, muttering under her breath, departed in search of a sophomore Nobel Prize winner; and the rest of us sat down to work at stories we'd already been assigned.

But I couldn't think of anything except how I was going to wade through the sea of letters Chip was holding for me — let alone how I was going to get them home.

I wandered casually over to Chip's desk and perched on the edge of it. Chip was going over a list of assignments, and there was no one else in our immediate vicinity.

"I'll bring them over to your house," he murmured, not even looking up from his list. "This afternoon — later. You go home now."

"Okay," I said, breathing a sigh of relief. Now I might have a fighting chance to get some English, French, and History homework done before I was inundated with two hundred envelopes full of other people's problems.

I was pawing through my cluttered locker in search of my French book when Marty materialized at my elbow.

"I was just coming to see if you wanted a ride home."

"Sure," I said, finally extricating my French book. I booted the assorted debris back into the bottom of my locker with my toe and slammed the door shut. I thought I heard something go "crunch" but I couldn't be sure.

Marty shook his shaggy head. "Aren't you ever going to clean that thing out?"

"When I graduate," I said airily.

We had hardly settled into his car when he sprang it on me.

"Come on now, Carrie, who's Lovey Hart? You must know. You're on the paper."

Startled, I jerked sideways and tried to mask my surprise by busily shifting the books on my lap. I looked straight out through the windshield to avoid Marty's eyes.

"It's a big secret, Marty," I said. "Nobody on the paper knows. Except Chip — and Lovey Hart, of course."

"I don't know how you can keep a secret like that."

No, it isn't easy to keep a secret like that, I silently agreed. And the hardest part was not being able to brag.

I mean, here was the most popular column ever to appear in the *Lincoln Log* (not that there had ever been much competition, to be perfectly truthful); here I was, the journalistic sensation of the decade, my name a household word (or schoolhold word) — only it wasn't *my* name, and all the fame and adulation that was rightfully mine couldn't be claimed. I felt vaguely like a mother who puts her son up for adoption, only to discover later that the child she can never acknowledge has become the President of the United States.

Frustrated, that's how I felt. And cheated. And just a little bit as if I had a split personality.

When we pulled up in front of my house, I

jumped out of the car and slammed the door. I leaned toward the window to say good-bye, but Marty, instead of waving and driving off, got out of the car and followed me up the walk.

"Maybe I'll come in for a while," he said comfortably.

Oh, no, not today! What if Chip were to show up while Marty was there? I mean, Marty might not be all that clever at spotting subtleties, but it did not exactly take a genius to figure out the only possible explanation for Chip coming over to my house with a shopping bag full of letters.

"I have a pile of work to do," I said weakly.

"Yeah, so do I. Look, we'll put on a couple of records, do it together, okay?"

So much for the "pile of work" gambit.

He went back to the car and reached in for his books, then followed me into the house.

My parents and Jen were standing in the middle of the living room as we entered. Apparently they froze on hearing the front door open, because the three of them seemed suspended in varying postures of hostility. Jen had her hands on her hips and her chin jutted out as if she were daring someone to punch it. My father stood with his arms folded, glaring at my mother, who sat on the edge of the piano bench looking disgusted with the whole business.

"Pay no attention to us," I said cheerfully, steering Marty down the hall toward the kitchen. "Just passing through."

"Carrie!" Jen shrieked. "You can give them your unprejudiced opinion!"

"Oh, no you don't," I called back. "Whatever this fight is about, I'm not involved."

"It's not a fight, it's merely a discussion," my father said coolly, trying to maintain his reputation for calm, guidance-counselor-like objectivity. After all, Marty was there, and it wouldn't look at all right for Dad to get hysterical, the way normal people do, in front of one of his students.

"The hell it is," my mother retorted feelingly.

"Carrie!" Jen's voice was shrill and desperate.

I sighed, threw Marty an apologetic glance, and backtracked to the field of conflict.

"Am I too young for a coed pajama party?" Jen demanded.

"*What?*" I exploded into something very near hysterics. *I* was too young for a coed pajama party, I thought fleetingly, as I fought for self-control. Jen was furious at my reaction.

"Stop laughing at me!" she howled. "It's not funny."

"I'm not laughing at *you*." I choked. "I'm just laughing at the — *idea*." I looked over toward my father for approval. He nodded. I had obeyed Rule Number One: Never criticize the person, criticize the action.

"*They* said I couldn't go," Jen snarled. She narrowed her eyes and peered at our parents as if they were microscopic specimens of some particularly odious bacteria. "And they can't give me one good reason."

"Oh, I imagine they can," I said gently.

"Whose side are you *on*?" she cried.

"Nobody's. I'm unprejudiced, remember?" Unforunately, to Jen the only valid unbiased opinion is one that supports her own argument.

"Jen," my mother said firmly, "pajama parties are for one sex only."

"But *why*?"

"Jennifer!" my father thundered. "Don't put on that dumb act with me!"

You could almost hear the sharp "Crack!" as my father broke Rule Number One.

"Marty?" Jen whimpered, turning to the one last potential ally in the room. Jen loves Marty. I'm not sure whether it's a crush, or whether she looks on him as her big brother; but ever since he rescued an abandoned kitten from the tree in front of our house, Marty has been an unqualified hero in Jen's eyes. As it turned out, she didn't get to keep the kitten because she's allergic to them, but that hadn't diminished Marty's prestige.

Marty, who'd been listening to the whole thing with, I sensed, barely suppressed guffaws, shook his head.

"I never heard of a coed pajama party," he said. "See, the thing with a coed pajama party is people might tend to call it an orgy."

"Oh!" Jen gasped angrily. "Oh, you!" Sputtering with anger at Marty's disloyalty, she stormed upstairs.

At which moment the doorbell rang.

Oh, no! Oh, no, I prayed, this is not Chip with

the letters. This is the Fuller Brush man. This is a lady collecting for Asthma. This is —

Jen raced back downstairs and flung open the front door before anyone else could reach it. She always races to answer the door, hoping it's someone for her. A good fifty percent of the time it is.

"Carrie home?" I heard and knew the sinking feeling that accompanies impending disaster.

Jen stalked back to the living room and stared icily in my general direction.

"It's for you."

FOUR

I went to the front door, hoping Marty would co-
operate by remaining in the living room and
making small talk with my parents.

Vain hope! He trailed behind me like an obe-
dient dog who's been told to heel.

"Oh, hi, Chip," he said brightly.

There stood Chip on the doorstep, shopping
bag and all. Was it my imagination, or did he
actually go slightly pale under what was left of
his summer tan?

It was probably my imagination, because he
recovered almost instantly.

"Hi, Marty. How's the team coming?"

"Really good. We're a little light on our defensive line, but —"

I tuned them out. They might as well have

been speaking Urdu, for all I could comprehend of the discussion. Sooner or later Chip was going to remember there had been a reason for his coming to my door with a bag full of letters, and have to figure out a way of explaining his presence without any reference to the truth.

"Carrie!" my mother called. "Don't stand there at the door — ask your friend in."

I tuned back to the football discussion, but Chip was saying, "That's okay, I'll only stay a minute. I came to get those galley proofs you had the other day, Carrie."

I looked at him blankly. I had no galley proofs — there weren't any galley proofs yet on this issue — there weren't even enough finished stories to make up one page of galley proofs. Besides which, it was absolutely against *Log* policy to take proofs home at all.

It probably didn't take me as long as it seemed to catch on. I stopped myself from exclaiming, "Oh, *those* galley proofs!" just in time.

"Oh, Chip, I forgot all about them," I said contritely.

"I know you did. I kept reminding you to bring them back."

"They're right in my desk. I'll get them now." I started slowly up the stairs, realizing suddenly that I was going to have to come back downstairs with something in my hand that looked vaguely like galley proofs, but Chip followed me up the steps, talking a mile a minute about column inches and slugging headlines.

"Marty, get something to eat," I called down. "This'll only take a minute."

"If your desk is anything like your locker," he called back, "I'll have time for a ten-course Chinese banquet."

Chip came into my room and I shut the door.

"What's he doing here?" he hissed. "I told you I'd be over."

"Well, why did you bring that stupid shopping bag right up to the door? How did you know who'd answer?"

"I assumed you had the sense to be waiting for me," he said coldly. He took some papers out of the bag, and I opened my bottom desk drawer.

"Just dump them in here," I said. "We'll put something back in the bag to make it look full again."

He hurriedly tossed the letters into the drawer, but they wouldn't all fit (Marty was right about my desk drawers) so we shoved them into two other drawers too, and I slammed them shut. I opened and closed all the drawers in my desk, to make it sound as if I were frantically searching for the proofs, if anyone happened to be listening.

I grabbed some paperback books and magazines and threw them in the shopping bag.

"Don't forget to give those back," I said.

"This is a fine time to worry about property rights," he growled. He thrust the extra papers he'd brought back on top of the books and picked up the shopping bag.

33

Just at that moment, the irrelevant — and certainly ill-timed — thought occurred to me that Chip was really very attractive. His hair was sort of dark blond and his eyes deep brown and intense. He was lean and serious-looking in contrast to Marty's broad-shouldered, husky blandness.

"All right, I'm going," he said, still sounding irritated. It was painfully obvious that he was having no irrelevant thoughts about me.

I followed him back downstairs. My parents and Jen were no longer in the living room, which was the first break I'd had all day.

But as Chip headed for the door, Marty emerged from the kitchen, a chicken leg in one hand and a Coke in the other.

"Find them?"

"Yeah," Chip replied. "See you."

"What's the matter with him?" Marty asked as Chip let himself out.

"I think he went into shock when he saw my desk drawers," I answered flippantly. "The idea of his precious proofs buried in the midst of the rubble was too much for him. Well, maybe now we can finally get some work done."

I'd no sooner started reading the Lovey Hart letters that evening when Chip phoned.

"Look, this is ridiculous," he said, without any silly preliminaries like "Hello" or "I'm sorry I snarled at you."

"Yeah," I agreed, "we've got to stop meeting like this."

"It isn't funny, Carrie. We're going to get so hung up on the mechanics of the damn thing, we'll have no time for anything else."

"What do you mean, 'we'?" I snapped. "I'm the one who's going to do all the work. Did you weigh that pile of letters? In the time it'll take to get through them I could polish off *War and Peace*."

"Writing it or reading it?" he asked, sounding amused.

"Both," I retorted.

"All right, look, what's your locker number?"

"376B. Why?"

"What's the combination?"

"18 right, 41 left, 5 right. *Why?*"

"Just a minute. 18, 41, 5. Okay. I'm going to take an old blue looseleaf, stick all the letters in there, and leave them for you in your locker. When you see the notebook there, just take it home with you, take out the letters, and bring it back the next day. Put it right back in your locker."

"It's brilliant, Chip," I said sincerely. "Except, people know it's my locker. I mean, what if Marty sees you, or Claudia? Sometimes they wait for me there."

"Believe me," he said feelingly, "they won't see me."

"Well. Okay, if you say so. But I'm beginning to feel more like a double agent for the CIA than a wise old mother figure."

"Neither image exactly fits you," Chip muttered.

Dear Lovey Hart,
    I am almost fourteen years old, and my mother will only let me go out with a group. She says I can't go out alone with a boy, especially if he has a car. This boy I really like has been asking me out, but he hates going with other couples, and only wants to take me out alone. I don't understand why he feels that way, but _am_ I too young to go out alone with him?

                                Puzzled

Dear Puzzled,
    If you don't understand why he wants to be alone with you, YES.

"Carrie?"

I leaped up from my desk, grabbed the first thing I laid my hands on, and dropped it on top of the letter I'd been working on.

Jennifer, having apparently either materialized out of thin air, like ectoplasm, or crept silently in on little flat feet, peered with thinly disguised suspicion at the apple-green gym suit lying on my desk.

"What are you doing?" she asked, with studied innocence.

"Oh, just some homework." I tried to sound casual. She didn't fall for my casual any more than I fell for her innocence.

"Why'd you cover it up?"

Why'd I cover it up? Good question. I sought frantically for an answer that would satisfy a cunning eleven-year-old and couldn't even come up with an explanation that would sound reasonable to a slow second-grader.

But Jen didn't wait for an explanation.

"I heard you and that boy in here before," she said. "You were whispering."

I fought back a gasp. What had she heard? What had we said? How much incriminating knowledge had she filed away in her head?

"You were eavesdropping!"

"I was not! I just *happened* to be walking past your door and heard you whispering, that's all."

She took a step toward me. I backed against the desk and tried to lean casually on it, one elbow resting on the gym suit. It was a ridiculous position, unnatural and uncomfortable, and Jen's look of scorn could have curdled milk.

"Well, what do you want then?" I asked. "You weren't speaking to me at all at dinner. Are we friends again?"

"Friends stick up for each other," Jen said sullenly. "Friends don't keep secrets from each other."

"They also respect one another's privacy," I pointed out.

"Maybe," Jen went on, as if she hadn't even heard me, "some secrets aren't as secret as some people think."

37

And with that she stalked out of my room.

Even if she hadn't put it too clearly, there was no mistaking the tone of her voice.

It was definitely threatening.

FIVE

Dear Lovey Hart,
        I am desperate. I love a man
who is old enough to be my father.
I worship him from afar. Do you
think there is any hope for a relationship between us?

                                    G.C.

Dear G.C.,
        Not unless he wants to adopt
you.

"You sure livened up this paper," Claudia said.
"You livened it up so much I can hardly find any
news in it."

Terry languished on Claude's bed, gazing va-
cantly at the ceiling. Her long hair cascaded like
a waterfall over the edge of the bed, and her slim

arms seemed flimsy and unsubstantial. She looked as if she might pine away from unrequited love before the afternoon was out, and I couldn't help an occasional nervous glance in her direction, just to assure myself she was still with us.

Claudia, cross-legged on the floor, ignored her as she hunched over the latest issue of the *Log*. She shook her dark, curly head disapprovingly as she flipped the pages.

"Look at this: 'Uncensored Thought of a Hockey Puck' by Jessie Krause?"

"Yeah, well, Jessie tried to come up with something — whimsical."

"Whimsical?" shrieked Claudia. "Carrie, it's positively sickening. And where, for God's sake, are the hockey scores? I mean, who won the game?"

"Jessie kind of got carried away with the poetry of it all, and forgot about covering the game," I explained. "Chip was a little annoyed about that — "

"And 'Osborne Krupnick'?" Claudia demanded, pointing to Cindy's Student of the Month column, which was headed by a very fuzzy picture of *someone*.

" 'Osborne Krupnick,' " she read aloud, " 'who emigrated to this country during the recent upheavals in Bosnia-Herzegovina, combines the intellect of the dedicated research scientist with the heart of a committed philanthropist. When he isn't collecting stray animals to employ in his research on the nutritional habits of the piranha, a huge tank of which he keeps in his basement laboratory, he serves as a member of the Board of Directors of the local ASPCA.' Carrie, that's ridiculous!"

"Claude," I sighed, "whatever happened to your sense of humor?"

She looked puzzled. "You mean, it's meant to be ridiculous?"

"Of course. There *is* no Osborne Krupnick. Cindy made him up."

"But Carrie, this is supposed to be a *newspaper*, not *Mad* magazine! How can you just make up — "

"Claude, will you stop? First you complain because the paper's dull, now you complain because it's lively. What do you want? And stop picking on me!" I added bitterly. "I only *work* there!"

"Lovey Hart says," Terry began abruptly, her voice distant and dreamy, "that you should let someone know if you like them, because they might be liking you all the time, and if you're too shy to ever tell each other, you'll never know what Might Have Been."

"Terry," I said nervously, "I think she was talking about a sophomore and a junior, not a student and a teacher."

"But the principle is still the same," Terry pointed out mildly.

Claudia and I exchanged worried looks — only my look must have been more worried than hers. I had a terrible feeling that I was going to be responsible for something I wanted no part of being

41

responsible for, and the thought was frightening.

"Don't you remember what she said to the girl who had a crush on a man old enough to be her father?" I demanded.

"Oh, that," she scoffed, as if the situation had no relation to her problem at all.

"You're not," Claudia said carefully, "thinking of doing anything . . . drastic?"

"If you mean like slashing my wrists," Terry said, "certainly not."

"No, no, I didn't mean *that*. I meant like — well, letting him *know* . . ."

Terry just smiled, an enigmatic, Mona Lisa smile, and let her eyes drift back to the ceiling.

I bit my lip and tried to think of something to say to discourage Terry from whatever it was she had in mind. Frantically I searched for an argument sound enough to refute the Lovey Hart principle which Terry had so ardently embraced. I knew I had to do something — say something — I knew there had to be a flaw in Lovey's — I mean *my* — logic somewhere, and I had to find it before Terry went off and made a fool of herself, or worse, in front of the one person she cared about.

"Terry," I said desperately, "when two people are equals — I mean, you know, peers — it's different from when they're — *not* equals."

Claudia frowned at me, trying to figure out what I was getting at.

"It's not the same with everyone. You have to know who you can approach, and who you can't."

"That's silly," Terry murmured. "How do you know unless you try?"

I looked helplessly at Claudia, but she just shrugged her shoulders and shook her head in defeat.

"But, Terry, sometimes it's best not to try," I went on hurriedly. "Sometimes the risks of getting — hurt — are too high."

"To live is to take risks," Terry said dreamily, sounding very much like a quotation from a Do-It-Yourself Psychology Primer.

I felt like pounding my fists into her. She was barely listening as it was, and I knew I was wasting my breath giving advice; ironically enough, she'd already *taken* my advice. The patient had swallowed the medicine prescribed for someone else — and now the doctor was beginning to feel sick herself.

"I've gotten some initial reaction to the *Log's* new image," Chip began the meeting. He looked strained.

"First the good news!" shouted Bob Teal.

"Okay," agreed Chip, with a slight, insecure grin. "The good news is that people are reading it."

"Yay," Bob said, sarcastically.

"What's the bad news?" asked Jessie.

"The bad news is, they don't like what they're reading," he said ruefully.

As if a small volcano had erupted, the staff

burst into a chorus of angry shouts and belligerent questions.

Chip held up his hand for quiet.

"We might," he admitted painfully, "have gone a little overboard. Maybe I carried a good idea to extremes — "

Mr. Gross, who had been sitting in the back of the room, unobtrusive as usual, interrupted him.

"I think what Chip means," he said gently, "is that we haven't gotten quite the right *mix* yet. It's just a matter of balance, between features and straight reportage — of course, striking that balance isn't the easiest thing in the world . . ."

By the time the meeting broke up, the incipient mutiny had been averted, and most of the staff was ready to forgive Chip for leading them astray.

But apparently no one was as hard on Chip as Chip himself, and as the kids gathered up their stuff and drifted off to various assignments, a look of heavy depression settled on his face.

Mr. Gross patted Chip on the shoulder and said something to him that was apparently meant to be consoling. Chip nodded glumly and Mr. Gross patted his shoulder again and left. Chip and I were now alone in the room, but I might as well have been one of the desks for all the attention he paid me.

And I did want Chip to pay attention to me. Ever since that afternoon when he'd been in my room, thoughts of Chip had been popping into my mind at the oddest moments. At first I hadn't paid too much attention to them.

But after several weeks of working on the *Log*, those thoughts were increasing in direct proportion to the amount of time I spent in the same office with him. I discovered that I liked his voice — so firm and assured — and that he had the sort of smile that you can't help smiling back at. I also discovered that, for some reason, being near Chip felt a whole lot different from being near Marty.

But what could I do about all this? Nothing. Lovey Hart had said, "Let someone know if you like him."

Humph. That was easy for Lovey Hart to say.

I watched Chip sorting papers, collecting his material in several little piles; he still wore that look of gentle despair, and I had this urge to put my arms around him and tell him that everything would be all right.

But of course that was out of the question. I sighed and picked up my books.

"Well, I guess I'll get going," I announced.

Chip looked up, as if surprised I was still there.

"Oh, yeah," he said absently. "So long."

I glanced out the window. It was gray and drizzly, a depressing afternoon to walk home alone.

Wouldn't it be nice, I thought, if Chip offered to drive me home?

"What a rotten day," I remarked.

"Sure is," he agreed. Of course, *he* wasn't referring to the weather.

"Look at that *rain*," I went on, as if the misty drizzle was, in fact, going to produce an unprecedented demand for arks.

"You staying long?" I asked, since Chip seemed unmoved by the possibility of forty days of rain. It was not very subtle, I admit, but what with Chip's preoccupation, it was plain that subtlety would get me nothing but a soggy walk home. Alone. I was more concerned with the alone part than the getting wet part, but I certainly didn't want Chip to realize that.

"No," he said, "I guess I'm done." He picked up his stuff and waited for me to walk out the door in front of him so he could turn out the lights and shut up the office.

"Need a ride?" he asked, with little enthusiasm. He probably hadn't heard a word I said.

"That would be great." I tried to strike the right tone — somewhere between overjoyed and casual. "It's so crummy out."

"Oh," he said, sounding as if he'd just emerged from a winter of hibernation, "is it raining?"

On the short ride home I began to feel almost invisible. Chip talked, but he was talking mostly to himself, and I seemed to serve no other purpose than to comment "Um-hm" or "Right" at the proper intervals.

If I'd expected Chip to suddenly turn to me,

at a red light or something, and murmur, "You know, I never realized . . ." (and to be honest, that's exactly what I'd hoped would happen) I might just as well have walked home.

Maybe the grapevine was right, and Chip simply had no interest in entangling alliances; or maybe I was just not the alliance he wanted to entangle himself with. Or maybe, now was simply an inauspicious time to even *think* about all this.

"Want to come in?" I asked halfheartedly. "I can make you some cocoa, or tea, or something."

I didn't know why I bothered. He hadn't even taken his hands off the steering wheel as he waited for me to let myself out of his car. Ingrained courtesy, I suppose, painstakingly taught to me by my mother at a time when I preferred to dump buckets of sand on boys rather than ask them to tea parties. I later realized that you got more attention by dumping sand on them than by plying them with tea — in a manner of speaking — but by then the habit of politeness had become firmly rooted, and there was no going back.

"Okay," Chip said unexpectedly. He turned off the ignition and got out of the car. For a moment I was too surprised to do anything but stand dumbly by the side of the car; then I recovered what little composure I'd had to begin with and led Chip up the walk to the house.

Jennifer hurtled down the stairs when she heard us come in, and stopped short when she saw who was with me.

47

"Oh, hi, Carrie," she purred. I didn't care for her tone of voice at all. Had she been two years younger she would have been taunting, "Carrie has a boy friend, Carrie has a boy friend," and while she wasn't literally saying the words, her voice had that same unmistakable undertone.

But Chip didn't seem to notice her any more than he'd noticed anything else since the *Log* meeting.

"I'm going to make some cocoa," I told her, dropping my books on the stairs. I didn't ask her to join us, although it was obvious she expected an invitation. Courtesy, I reflected, can be carried too far.

"Mom's out shopping," she remarked, following Chip and me into the kitchen. The lack of a formal invitation wasn't going to deter her.

"I'll have some too," she said, planting herself firmly on a kitchen chair and threatening to take root.

"Would you rather have tea, Chip?" I asked. I pointedly ignored Jen.

"No, cocoa's fine," he said, leaning against the refrigerator.

I gave Jen a long, meaningful look that — roughly translated into words — said, "Get out of here!" but she chose not to understand it. I didn't want to say outright that she should get lost, because I didn't want Chip to know I was that eager to be alone with him. She had me over a barrel.

At that moment my mother walked in, loaded with bundles.

"Hi," she said cheerfully, dropping the bags on the table.

"Mom, this is Chip. He's the editor of the *Log*. We were just going to have some cocoa." I gave *her* a meaningful glance, and tilted my head ever so slightly toward Jen.

My mother is clever. Instantly grasping the situation, she said, "Well, I've got two more bags in the car to unload. Since I'm going to be kind of busy in here for a while, why don't you take Chip into the den, so no one gets in anyone's way?"

I smiled gratefully and showed Chip where the den was. Jen started to follow us in, but my mother said, "You can help me, Jennifer. Would you bring the rest of the stuff inside, please?"

Jen grumbled, but obeyed.

Hurriedly I whipped up some cocoa and practically ran back to the den, where Chip was sitting on the couch, idly thumbing through yesterday's paper.

As I sipped my cocoa, I realized I had been in a little bit too much of a hurry. It was barely lukewarm.

It didn't bother me. Chip hadn't noticed anything else that afternoon; he wasn't about to be aroused by substandard cocoa.

"Chip," I began gently, feeling the need to somehow yank him out of his mood, "don't you think you're taking this too hard? I mean, it's just one issue — and instead of thinking about how to improve the paper in the future, you're dwelling

49

on the things you think we did wrong in the past. That's very destructive, you know."

I sounded just like Lovey Hart, I thought.

"I know," he sighed. He put down his cup and hunched over on the couch, elbows on his knees. I wanted to run my hand down his back. I wanted *very much* to run my hand down his back. So I clenched my hands together and tried to think of something else to say. Of course his moodiness intrigued me. I'd never known he was moody, and the revelation made him even more appealing. For some reason I equate moodiness with great depth of feeling, way beyond anything your average cheerful optimist is capable of.

But while a brooding, intense boy makes the heart beat faster, he also puts a simultaneous strain on the brain, because you are frantically trying to think of something to say to make him stop brooding, which is an outright contradiction, but true, nevertheless.

"I don't like to *fail*," he said bitterly.

"Chip, you didn't fail!" I protested. "Why do you put it that way?"

"Because that's the way it is."

"Ridiculous!" I moved closer to him on the couch. I'll touch his hand, I thought. Gently. I'll just reach over and rest my hand on top of his hand, a friendly, comforting gesture.

There's nothing to be afraid of. I touch people all the time, I told myself. Just a friendly pat.

I unclenched my fists and started to raise my hand.

He leaned back against the couch, clasping his hands behind his head. If I let my fingers continue on their present course, I would be gently touching his knee.

I snatched my hand back.

"The thing is," he said, ignorant of the internal battle I had just waged (and lost), "it's so hard to get any life into the same old garbage. It's a matter of style, I guess. I can't make *them* into brilliant writers, so I went and tried to make the *news* more brilliant. And then it stopped being news, and turned into — oh, hell, I don't know. I guess Mr. Gross is right; we haven't got the right balance."

"Of course," I soothed. "That's all it is. It's just a matter of trial and error — "

"But there's no room for error!" he exclaimed. "Don't you see that?"

I inched away from him, startled by his intensity and his rigid attitude.

"No," I said, confused. "I don't see that. You've only been editor for two months. Why do you expect to be able to turn out a perfect paper right off the bat? No one expects it."

"*I* expect it," he muttered.

"But that's ridiculous."

He sagged, and his body seemed to go limp. He dropped his arms at his sides; without even stopping to think, and with no motive other than trying to get his attention, I grabbed his wrist and squeezed hard.

"Nobody's perfect the first time they try! Or

the second time," I added, before he could remind me he'd done two issues.

He stared at me, then looked down at his trapped wrist. I snatched my hand away as if I'd been burned and self-consciously avoided his eyes.

"Well, I better get going," he said, and stood up. I slowly got to my feet and took a deep breath, as if to steady myself.

"Thanks for the cocoa."

"You're quite welcome." It came out colder than I'd intended.

Ever courteous, I walked him to the door. He went right through the kitchen, past my mother and sister, without a word, as if he hadn't even seen them. Jen frankly stared.

I opened the front door for him.

"See you," he said shortly. He was halfway down the walk by the time I realized I hadn't replied.

As I shut the door behind him, a wave of defeat washed over me. Whatever — if anything — he felt about me, he'd made it perfectly obvious that I was resistible. In fact I was barely noticeable. Maybe he was so wrapped up in his own weird problems that he couldn't handle any other "relationships" — but then again, maybe he just didn't want a relationship with *me*. Maybe if I'd been someone else, things would have worked out differently.

I told myself to forget it. To forget the whole afternoon and to forget Chip. He was just someone with whom I happened to work, and our relationship would be strictly business.

But the pain stayed right where it was. I made my way wearily upstairs to work on some Lovey Hart letters, hoping to take my mind off my own problems by plunging myself into the problems of other people.

It was ironic that the only person Lovey Hart couldn't advise was Caroline Wasserman.

SIX

Dear Lovey Hart:

I wrote to you before asking for advice about getting friends. I was the one who had been on drugs. Anyway, I had to write and tell you how grateful I am for your help, because what you told me to do really worked. I did what you said, and asked a person to come over after school and study with me. It was really hard the first time, because I felt very shy, but he said sure, and came, and we got to be good friends. And I did this a couple of times, and only one person refused, and he later on asked me to <u>his</u> house.

I feel really good now, and I want you to know that it's all because of you that my whole life is

changed. You don't have to print
this, or answer it or anything.
      I just wanted you to know.

                    Sincerely,
                    A Grateful Person

My eyes welled up with tears as I read the letter. I had to reread it three times, as if to reassure
myself that it was real. I had actually changed
someone's life! I had actually helped someone
with a serious problem to take his destiny in his
hands and create a new beginning for himself.
Me, Carrie Wasserman — Lovey Hart, really —
had done this, and I was so proud of the ac-
complishment, I felt like I would burst if I didn't
tell someone.

But there was no one to tell.

No one could ever know what I'd done. I was
a secret. Whatever help I gave would go unher-
alded. I was the anonymous benefactor of
troubled souls, curing neuroses with generous do-
nations of wit and wisdom. I liked being the
benefactor, but it was more difficult than ever to
resign myself to anonymity.

I could, I thought suddenly, call Chip. I had
a perfectly valid reason for talking to him, and it
was better to let him in on my elation than to
suddenly burst it out because I couldn't keep it
in anymore. After all, everyone needs a safety
valve. You can't expect to be superhuman, and
keep things bottled up inside you all the time.

At least, that's what I told myself *now*.

Since the "Afternoon of the Cocoa," I had been

very careful to maintain a strictly businesslike attitude around Chip. He never referred to our conversation, and neither did I. He was every bit as friendly as he ever was — and not one bit more so. I took my cue from him, and tried not to dwell on the fact that I'd hoped (maybe still was hoping) to be more than just friends.

There was no reason I couldn't call him — colleague-to-colleague — just to let him know how much of a success his column idea really was. He'd be glad to hear that someone had actually benefited from his determination to deal with serious as well as not-so-serious problems.

Besides, the work load was getting to me. There was still a small mountain of mail to go through, and even though Mr. Gross had, thank heaven, vetoed Chip's idea of replying personally to every letter, all the mail still had to be read.

I deserved a coffee break; I'd earned it, and I needed a brief respite from drudgery.

I reached for the phone on my desk and it rang as my hand touched the receiver.

"Hello?"

There was a short sniffle on the other end, then a barely suppressed moan. For a moment I toyed with the intriguing idea that it might be an obscene call from a severely depressed pervert, but the whimpered "Carrie?" dispelled that notion.

"Oh, Terry, not again!"

This was the fourth call in three days from Terry, who was going through an emotional crisis of epic proportions. She asked for my opinion, then ignored everything I said; begged for my sympathy, but refused to hear it; and kept me on the phone for upwards of an hour each time, as my patience wore thinner and letters and homework piled up in front of my glazed eyes.

"Carrie, I *have* to talk to you!"

Didn't she always? Wasn't it always a matter of life and death?

"Terry," I said firmly, "I just don't have time now."

"But, Carrie, it's —"

I felt cold, cruel, heartless. But I also felt overwhelmed by work, my emotional bankroll already overdrawn by the pile of problems I'd already read through that evening, and with needs of my own which I felt sure the call to Chip would satisfy.

"I'm sorry, Terry. I can't talk to you now. I'll see you tomorrow, okay?"

No response but a sniffle.

"Okay, Ter?" Now don't weaken, I told myself. Stay firm.

"All right." He voice was dull, leaden. I ignored, or tried to, the heavy sigh.

"So long," I said, and hung up.

I shook my head as if to dispel Terry's grim mood, which had begun to infect me, but I couldn't quite recapture the elation I'd felt earlier, after reading the letter from "Grateful."

I dialed Chip's number, which I had somehow happened to memorize, and waited for someone to answer.

Jen knocked on my door, and without waiting for a "Come in" came in and flopped on my bed.

"Who's that on the phone?" she asked, just as Chip's voice answered "Hello?" and just as I realized that the Lovey Hart letters were in plain sight on my desk.

"Hi, Chip, it's Carrie, can you hold on a minute?"

I covered the mouthpiece with my hand and glared at Jen.

"Could I have a little privacy *please*?"

"I'm sorry," she said haughtily. "I just wanted to borrow some looseleaf paper. I'll wait till you're finished."

"Wait elsewhere."

"Well!" she said, and stomped out of my room, slamming the door.

I was beginning to feel like the emergency truck dispatcher at the Chicago Fire. I sighed, and removed my fingers from the mouthpiece.

"Chip, I had to tell you about this letter," I began.

"What letter? Is anyone else there?"

"No, of course not." But I lowered my voice and tried to keep one ear open for Jen, who might "just happen" to walk by the door.

"Remember the letter from the kid who was on drugs? In the first issue?"

"Oh, yeah, I remember."

"Well, listen to this." I read him the letter, barely raising my voice above a whisper, so that he had to interrupt with "What?" a couple of

58

times. But when I finished, his voice brimmed over with enthusiasm.

"Hey, that's really something!"

Picturing his delighted smile was just the antidote I'd needed. Immediately I forgot whatever guilt feelings I'd acquired from brushing Terry off, and my emotional barometer zoomed.

"See, we really helped someone," he crowed. "I told you we shouldn't ignore the serious stuff."

"I guess you were right," I agreed. "I never realized I had this innate talent for problem-solving."

"Like father like daughter," he said lightly.

"I guess so," I grinned.

"Well. That's really great. Congratulations."

"Thanks."

"Well." Long pause. "Going to the game Saturday?"

"What — oh, the football game." Was he going to ask me to go with him? I clutched the phone tighter. Marty had asked me to go and watch him, because the first-string quarterback or cornerback — or whatever it was Marty was the second or third string of — was injured, and probably wouldn't play very much. I hadn't really wanted to go, but if Chip wanted me to go *with* him, well, that was a different story.

I forgot completely about my strictly business attitude and waited, heart beating just a little faster with expectancy, for him to suggest it.

"I don't know," I said finally, after waiting a few heartbeats for him to say *something*...

"Well, maybe I'll see you there then. Take it easy."

I dropped the phone back on the hook distastefully, as if it were leprous. I'd made the stupid mistake of interpreting small talk as a prelude to something bigger, and I was angry with myself. How much more obvious did it have to be that Chip was *not interested* in me before I'd stop breaking all those resolutions I'd made to be not interested in *him*?

A sudden creak in the floor outside my door roused me and I practically knocked my chair over as I leaped up and flung the door open.

Someone disappeared into the bathroom just as I peered down the hall. The bathroom door slammed shut. I looked in Jen's room. She wasn't there.

Frowning, I removed a few sheets of looseleaf paper from my notebook and took them into her room, where I dropped them next to some books on her bed. Could she have been listening to the conversation with Chip? And if she had, what had she heard?

She might have heard me reading him the letter, that's what she might have heard, I thought grimly. And although she hadn't been particularly Mata Hari-ish since the day Chip drove me home, there was still the nagging fear at the back of my mind that she was suspicious of me. There was no arguing the fact that she *had* acted before as if she had something on me — or thought she did; she'd practically said so when she talked about "some people's secrets." What was driving me crazy was, when was she going to spring whatever it was she was going to spring? What was she waiting for? And why did she want to have something to spring in the first place?

SEVEN

Dear Lovey Hart:
My boyfriend spends all his
time and money on a 1962 Jaguar he's
fixing up. He never <u>takes</u> me anyplace in it — if I want to see him
at all I usually have to sit in the
garage and hand him wrenches and
things while he works on the car.

I'm getting sick and tired of
playing second fiddle to that old
hunk of junk, but I can't seem to
get through to my boyfriend. He's
always underneath that car, hammer-
ing away at something or other.

What can you do with a guy
like that?

Fed Up

Dear Fed Up:
Trade him in on a new model.

"GIVE ME AN *L*!"

"L!"

"GIVE ME AN *I*!"

"I!"

"GIVE ME AN *N*!"

"N!"

"GIVE ME A *C*!"

"See, there's Marty," Claudia said, pointing to a bunch of Lincoln uniforms with people who all looked the same in them.

"I can't tell one broad shoulder from another," I said carelessly. I scouted the bleachers for a glimpse of Chip.

"You go by the numbers, dummy. They're in the program."

I hadn't looked at the program.

"He's number 14."

"I glanced back at the cluster of arms, legs, and shoulders, all huddled together as if for warmth.

"Oh, yeah, I see him," I said. "I have a really terrific view of his back."

"And by the time we find a place to sit," Claudia pointed out, "we'll be 'way up there, and you'll be lucky to see the top of his head."

Claudia, propelling a glum, silent Terry around like a mother directing a three-year-old through a supermarket, started to climb up the bleachers, scanning the tiers for a place to sit.

"Claude, over there!" I shouted, but she ignored me and kept climbing, pushing Terry in front of her, and looking, looking all the while.

She passed up at least four perfectly good spots

until she found what she wanted, in the next to the last row of bleachers.

"Claude, we could have had much better seats —" I stopped myself in midsentence. Claudia was edging her way down the row to where there was a gap perhaps wide enough to seat two rail-thin fashion models or one overweight child. While it was perfectly obvious that the three of us normal, healthy, well-fed girls would never squeeze into that space, it was also perfectly obvious that on the other side of that space was Chip.

Claudia is very perceptive, but she's no mind reader and I hadn't said a word to her about Chip, except when we talked about my work on the *Log*. So no matter how perceptive she was, I couldn't imagine how she could have picked up any of those vibrations I'd been so careful to keep hidden.

But suppose she had; if so, why was she climbing over people's feet, *ahead* of Terry and me, and sitting down next to Chip *herself*? Why hadn't she let *me* go in first?

The entire bench shifted as we wedged ourselves into a place too small to accommodate us, and you could hear the mutters and snarls even over the general roar of the spectators. I pictured someone on one end of the bench suddenly being shoved off the edge, and plunging down the side of the stands to his death, but since there was no bloodcurdling scream, I relaxed.

Or relaxed as much as I could, considering that

I had to hunch my shoulders, lean forward, and hold my arms so close togther that my elbows scraped each other. I glanced over at Claude, who was talking animatedly to Chip. Terry, next to me, was staring straight ahead, looking at nothing, hearing nothing, caring about nothing.

It was going to be a fun afternoon.

Chip spotted me and waved. Bob Teal, sitting next to him on the other side, leaned over and waved.

"Marty's starting," he shouted, cupping his hands to make his voice carry.

"Good!" I shouted back. I tried to return his smile. I'm afraid my attempt was slightly strained.

When we stood for the playing of the national anthem, I was carried to my feet by the shoulders wedged on either side of me. It's a good thing I didn't want to protest anything by keeping my seat; it would have been impossible.

Likewise, when the singing was over, I sat, by popular demand and group pressure. I imagined we must look like a giant row of paper dolls, all attached to one another at the elbow.

As the game started, I peered past Terry (who was perfectly lousy company) to Chip, who had his eyes glued to the line of players on the field. Claudia had her eyes glued on Chip.

I turned back toward the field and bit my lip as I gazed, unseeing, at the action. Was it possible, was it all possible, that Claudia — my best friend — wanted —

"YAY!"

"What happened?" I asked the boy sitting next to me.

"Klein carried for a first down."

That meant Marty had done something good. He'd expect me to have noticed. I was glad I asked.

But Claudia, who had never been in love, and Chip — well, maybe they had something in common at that.

How could she, I fumed silently. How could she *do* this to me?

"YAY!"

I was involuntarily carried to my feet as the rest of the crowd stood up, screaming. The wooden floor of the bleacher shook ominously, and I grabbed Terry's arm to steady myself.

We sat down.

I smiled helplessly at the boy next to me.

"Completed pass," he said, with only a slightly patronizing air. From the way he kept thumping his fists together I figured that was good.

"I really have to pay closer attention," I muttered apolegetically.

"It might help," he said.

Why shouldn't she go after Chip? I scolded myself. She had no idea, after all, that I wanted him. Or *had* wanted him, I amended. Because of course, now I was resigned to not having him, and it really shouldn't bother me in the least if Claudia went after him. Good luck to her, I thought. Why not? Maybe it was all for the best anyway.

I looked over at them again. Claudia now seemed to be sneaking glimpses of Chip out of the corner of her eye. Subtle. Chip didn't seem to be paying any attention to Claudia at all.

Good, I thought, and then, oh, no, I don't really mean that. After all, I should feel — but somehow I couldn't convince myself not to be glad that Claudia's initial campaign did not seem to be getting off the ground.

That's a very dog-in-the-manger attitude, I told myself. That's not a nice way to be at all.

At halftime, Chip went to get something to eat, and Claudia, who was supposed to be on a diet, developed a sudden and ravenous hunger for hot dogs, so of course, she went with him. She returned bearing goodies which Chip helped her carry.

"GIVE ME A *C*!"

"C!"

"GIVE ME AN *O*!"

"O!"

"GIVE ME AN *L*!"

"Oh, hell," I muttered, as my hot dog was knocked out of my hands and fell through the bleachers to the ground. It sort of figured, the way everything else had been going.

By this time there was nothing left for me to do but watch the game, and as the second half wore on, I found it really was not all that difficult to keep track of what was going on, provided you paid attention. It's simple enough: When Lincoln advanced toward the goalposts, that was good. When they kept the other team from advancing toward the other goalposts, that was good too. I knew that much, and of course I knew what a touchdown was, so I had no trouble once I kept my mind on the game.

When it was all over (we won), I battled my way out of the bleachers, followed by Terry and Claudia. The moment we were on terra firma again Claudia planted herself next to Chip, who had alighted from the stands right behind us.

"Marty played a good game," Bob said. "Maybe I ought to do a special feature interview with him for the next issue. You know, box it right next to the game write-up."

"He'll like that," I said absently. Claudia was hanging on to Chip as if they were Siamese twins. He said something to her but I couldn't hear what it was. She nodded.

"Carrie," she said, coming over to where Bob and I were standing, "Chip's going to drive me home. You don't mind, do you? I know you promised Marty to wait for him and I really don't feel like — waiting around."

I folded my arms together tightly to prevent myself from hauling off and slugging my so-called best friend in the eye. My heart hardened against her, and my scowl belied my words.

"I don't mind." Which is not easy to say between clenched teeth.

She searched my face for a moment, then shrugged and turned away.

"What about Terry?" I snapped. "You going to leave her here?"

Claude looked back at me again.

"What's the matter with you? Are you mad about something?"

Oh, certainly not. Why should I be mad? Just because my best friend has fastened herself like a leech to a boy I have to force myself not to think about — which is somewhat like telling myself that whatever I do, I must *not* think about oysters — is that any reason to be angry? If she wants to make a fool of herself falling all over a boy who's bound to cause her nothing but grief, why should I object?

No girl had ever enticed Chip into any gesture more passionate than a hearty handshake, but suppose — *just suppose* — that Claudia turned out to be the girl who could. It's all very fine to tell yourself not to care about a guy; it's another thing entirely to actually succeed in not caring. So no matter what I *told* myself, if Claudia managed to achieve some sort of relationship with Chip, that would mean she'd won and I'd lost. A crude way to put it, but true all the same. And only *I* knew we were in a contest.

"Mad? Why should I be mad?"

"Good," she said, not caring to probe any deeper at the moment: "Come on, Terry." She took Terry's arm and led her away. "Chip's going to drive us home." Zombielike, Terry complied.

They waved cheerily to me, leaving me by myself at the base of the stands as the area rapidly emptied out.

I was alone. I slumped down onto a first-row bleacher and waited for Marty to be finished changing and doing whatever it was football players did after a game. I resented everyone. I resented Marty, for asking me to come to the game; I was annoyed with myself for promising to wait for him afterward; I was resentful of Chip for offering to drive Claudia home; I was furious at Claudia for practically twisting Chip's arm to get him to ask her.

By the time Marty emerged from the locker room half an hour later, I was the biggest little bundle of resentments in the world. One hundred and five pounds of sheer irritation, wearing a strained smile and trying unsuccessfully to mask my true feelings with phony heartiness.

"How'd you like the game?" Marty asked, grinning broadly.

"It was better than I thought it would be," I said. "I really didn't have much trouble following it at all."

"See, I told you you'd like it, once you gave it a chance."

"I didn't exactly say I liked it," I corrected him gently. "I just said I sort of understood it."

"Well, understanding is the first step toward enjoyment," he said. He sounded pompous. I don't like pomposity.

"I suppose so."

He looked at me strangely. I was getting a lot

of strange looks today. I was getting pretty sick and tired of all those strange looks. I stared back, boldly, challengingly. I'm not at all sure what I was challenging him to, but it didn't matter, since he immediately changed the subject.

"So, where should we go to eat?" he asked.

And why was everybody suddenly so concerned about feeding me today, I wondered bitterly. Food for the body, when it was my soul that was starved.

When I shrugged disinterestedly he suggested, "How about Rocco's for pizza? A lot of the other guys are going there. Might be fun."

Oh, sure. Lots of fun. I could just see myself in the midst of a bunch of jocks and cheerleaders, leading everyone in the Lincoln fight song.

Rah-rah.

"What's the matter with you today?" Marty demanded. "The mood you're in, you'd think we lost."

"Maybe some of us did," I said mysteriously, picturing Chip and Claudia dropping Terry and Bob off first, then driving to Claudia's house alone, together.

"*What?* I wish you'd tell me what's on your mind," he said impatiently. "You're really acting weird."

"Take my word for it," I warned him, "you don't want to know." I took a deep breath and forced my "Good Old Carrie" mask back on.

"Now, let's get to Rocco's before all those happy halfbacks eat everything in sight — including the tables."

71

EIGHT

Dear Lovey Hart,
My problem is that girls don't
seem to think of me as anything more
than a "pal." I'm good-looking
enough, and I try to be agreeable
and pleasant, but they never treat
me like anything but a "nice guy."
I'm always willing to do what they
want to do, like if we go to the
movies I ask what they want to see,
etc., but no matter how much I try
to please them, they always act indifferent and uninterested in me.
What can I do to change this?

Everybody's Brother

Dear Brother,
Stop trying to please everyone
but yourself. Be more decisive, more

masterful. Don't be a doormat. When
you have respect for yourself,
others will have respect for you.
Girls are not turned on by wishy-
washy boys, and you are acting
wishy-washy. Spice up that "good
guy" approach with a dash of cave-
man, and the girls will see a whole
new you.

"All day," said Bob, as we settled into neigh-
boring desks for the *Log*'s staff meeting, "I've
been waiting to see someone dragging a girl
down the hall by her hair."

"Good grief," I said, startled, "has the battle of
the sexes come to *that*?"

"Didn't you read Lovey Hart's latest edict?"

"Oh, that." I'd practically forgotten what I'd
written by this time. "I hope he doesn't take it
quite so literally."

"Well, if he does, he may be in for a shock. I
can't picture any of the girls around here going
for the 'Me Tarzan, you Jane,' bit. The last time
I tried it Jane nearly decked me with a swift
right to the jaw. Of course," he added, his eyes
taking on a faraway look, "I was only thirteen at
the time . . ."

Chip rapped on the desk for attention.

"I think this latest issue is just about perfect."

He beamed at his staff.

We beamed back. Mutual admiration and good
fellowship permeated the atmosphere and I felt a
cozy glow of satisfaction. Chip's good moods, it
seemed, were as infectious as his bad moods.

"I think Mr. Gross was right about achieving the proper balance between straight news reporting and features, and I think in this issue we did it. Don't you, Mr. Gross?"

Mr. Gross removed the unlit pipe from between his teeth and laid it down on the desk before him.

"Yes," he agreed, "I think you did and I think the issue in general was quite good. I do have one comment to make though, concerning the sports reporting." Bob frowned and twisted around to face Mr. Gross, who sat in his usual spot at the back of the room.

"I'd like to see a more objective approach to the reporting of sports events, Bob. Your own reactions to the football game, for instance, should be in a separate opinion column, clearly labeled as opinion."

"You mean my bias is showing," Bob said.

"It's not *too* bad," said Mr. Gross, "but it's there. Subtle things, but nonetheless — I remember, for example, in the article about the Lincoln-Woodfield game, you said something like, 'Fortunately, Coleman was able to pass for a two-point conversion.' That 'fortunately' doesn't belong in the straight news story."

"Yeah, I see what you mean. I shouldn't be glad we won in the news story — just in my column."

Mr. Gross nodded and smiled. "That's it," he said.

"Anything else, Mr. Gross?" Chip asked.

He shook his head and put his pipe back in his mouth.

"Well, then, a couple of ideas. What we still need, I think, is something in the way of a regular feature that will stir up as much interest as the Lovey Hart column. You know what a success that's been, and it's because the kids look forward to it every issue. I'd like to have one or two more columns like that — things that would make regular *Log* readers out of the kids. We've had some ideas, but no one has come up with anything yet that's different enough to really catch on."

I couldn't help but notice that Chip had carefully avoided looking in my direction throughout this speech. It seemed awfully obvious to *me*; I wondered if anyone else had thought it too, or even thought about it at all?

"What about an astrology column?" Cindy suggested.

Chip frowned. "I don't know," he said uncertainly. "It seems to me you'd have to have somebody who really knew the field to be able to do that. If you're going to do it at all, you've got to be at least an amateur astrologer. Can any of you . . . ?"

He looked around as everyone shook their heads.

"Well, it was just a thought," Cindy shrugged.

"How about a gossip column?" suggested Al Ramirez, who was the photography editor. "The girls go for that."

Six of us girls in the room whirled around to glare at him. "Well they *do*," he said defensively.

"If we do," I said, "how come one of us didn't suggest it?"

Jessie leaned over and patted me on the shoulder. We exchanged satisfied smiles.

"The trouble with that is," Chip said, ignoring the minor scuffle, "the person who writes the column always writes about a small group of people she knows personally, so the thing has very limited appeal. All the columns like that I've ever seen keep having the same names in them, week after week. It gets to be like a little private club, you know, all exclusive and status-oriented. I really don't see what purpose it serves."

He looked around helplessly. "No other ideas?"

"A humor column?" Bob said. "Something like the political columnists do, but school-centered? You know, 'The Lighter Side of Lincoln.'"

"That's not a bad idea," Chip said thoughtfully. "You know, that's not a bad idea at all. Let's see, who could handle that?" He looked around the room, as if waiting for volunteers.

"Carrie could do it," Bob said. "She's funny."

No! I have enough to do! Chip must realize I couldn't handle another column.

Chip eyed me speculatively. "You *could* do it, Carrie," he said.

"But Chip, you write well, and you're the editor." Mine was the desperation of a drowning man grasping at a straw.

"I can't take on anything else," he said firmly. "I'm here every day as it is, working on this paper."

But I can't take on anything else either, I thought, knowing full well the drowning man was going under for the third time.

"Oh, you'll enjoy it," he said cheerfully. "And you'll have your own by-line every month." He sounded as if I were a squalling baby that he was pacifying with a piece of zwieback. See, look what I've got for the nice baby if she'll just shut up.

But, being me, there was a certain appeal in Chip's approach. (And being Chip, he probably realized it.) I did want to be recognized and praised for my work and the Lovey Hart column was not giving me the gratification I yearned for. Maybe this new column, with my name above it, would be as widely read and as popular as Lovey Hart. Maybe my *real* name would become a schoolhold word.

And maybe I could learn to write with both hands at once.

After the meeting I went to my locker to see if there were any letters in the blue notebook. As I bent down to pull it out, Claudia walked by. I snatched the notebook to my chest, covering it with my English text, but she didn't even break her stride as she passed me. Her mind was obviously elsewhere, or I was beneath her line of vision, or something, because looking neither right nor left she headed straight for the *Log* office.

I stood up slowly, watching her enter. Through the open door I could see her perch on the desk where Chip was talking to Mr. Gross. I kicked the locker door closed and stood there waiting to see what she would do. As she lingered to speak to Chip my anger grew. What right did she have to throw herself at him that way? Maybe I didn't have any valid reason to be jealous, but *I* was here first. After all, *I* was the one who worked on the paper. *I* was the one who was with him most. If she wanted to go after someone, why didn't she stick to someone in her own territory, like a nice fellow from Orchestra or the Mathletes? What right did she have to come barging into my activities trying to lure away the one person who was important to *me*?

I should have told her, I thought. I should have told her when I first felt this way about Chip, just as I've told her about almost everything else since we've been eleven. Then she would have kept hands off Chip and —

But would she have? I thought suddenly, bitterly. *Would she have?* Maybe she would have figured all's fair in love, etc., or every woman for herself, and thought that her crush on Chip was more important than our years of intimate friendship. Maybe all I would have accomplished by telling her would have been to leave myself vulnerable to humiliation if he chose her over me.

Dark thoughts chased one another through my mind as Mr. Gross left the room and Claudia put her head close to Chip's. I leaned back against my locker, my eyes squinted into little mean slits, watching the tête-à-tête. I clutched my books tightly, as if the pangs of anger and jealousy which threatened to erupt could be pressed back down again.

"'Bye, Carrie," said Mr. Gross pleasantly.

"So long," I whispered, barely managing to be polite.

Claudia showed no signs of finishing her business with Chip and going home. As a matter of fact, it looked as if she'd taken out a lease on the desk and planned to be there for the duration.

Another ride home, I thought sourly. It wasn't enough to make a fool of herself once; now she'll wait here till seven if that's how long he takes to get his work done, as long as she gets to ride home with him.

Well, I don't have to stay around and watch, I reminded myself. I don't have to stand here and make myself miserable just because my best friend is stabbing a knife through my heart.

I strode purposefully down the hall to the stairs. I had plenty of work to do: I had to study for an algebra test; I had a pile of Lovey Hart letters, plus a new column to think about; I had to read "The Fall of the House of Usher" for English; and if I had time after doing all of that, it was very possible that I would throw myself onto my bed and cry for a good, long time.

NINE

Dear Lovey Hart,
      Why is it I can get along with
everybody except my own family? All
we do is fight and argue all the
time, and I say rotten things that
I'm sorry for later. We treat
strangers better than we treat each
other.
      What can I do to improve rela-
tions with my parents?

                              Miserable

Dear Miserable,
      Treat them like strangers.

"Carrie, what *is* the matter?" demanded my
mother, as I succeeded in turning a normally
pleasant family dinner into a snarling session.

"Nothing!" I snapped, harpooning a french fry with my fork more viciously than Captain Ahab ever pursued Moby Dick. "What makes you think something's the matter?"

"Oh, I don't know," my mother said dryly. "I just get the feeling that all this sweetness and light you're treating us to isn't sincere."

"Leave her alone," my father advised. "When she wants to discuss it, she'll tell us. Until then, it's *her* problem."

"*Her* problem! Maybe *she* doesn't have a problem! Maybe *she* doesn't have anything to discuss!" I glowered at the three of them. Jen, who is too old to stick her tongue out at people, stuck it out at me.

"Then *she's* not human," my father said mildly. "Because everyone else has problems at one time or another."

"Did it ever occur to you," I retorted, "that this may be the 'one time' I don't?"

"Maybe she's going through menopause," Jen suggested.

My mother covered her mouth with her hand and my father clamped his lips together in a painfully obvious attempt to keep from smiling.

I didn't think it was funny at all.

"Someone," I said acidly, "ought to teach that child some manners."

"I'm not a child!" Jen shrieked.

"What are you, a grape?"

"Carrie." My mother's voice was cold. "I'm sorry if you're in a bad mood, but don't inflict it on the rest of us. I'm really getting fed up with your sarcasm and the constant bickering — ever since you came home it's been — "

"I wish everyone would stop saying I'm in a bad mood!" I yelled, leaping up from my chair. "I'm not in a bad mood! I feel just fine!"

I stormed out of the kitchen and up the stairs to my room. I slammed the door hard behind me.

I flung myself down at my desk and clenched my hands together. I am not going to cry. I am *not* going to cry. My breath came in little strangled gasps of anger as I fought to control myself.

I'm acting like a fool. Like a total, complete, and utter fool. Let Claudia play the fool; one fool is enough. We don't need two fools. Two fools is one fool too many. Maybe one fool is one fool too many.

My mind was running amok. I swiped savagely at the tears that had started to flow. I had work to do. Lots of work. I didn't have time for tears. Not now. Now I had to study, and ponder other people's problems, and give them magic solutions, and think up funny things to say in my new column. And, to add a cheerful note to the evening, read Poe.

No crying now. It was time to be funny. "The Lighter Side of Lincoln" by Carrie Wasserman.

"A funny thing happened on my way to the *Log* office. A girl came up to me and said, 'Would you chip in to help me get home?'" Chip in, get it? *Chip* in?

Hilarious. I'm going to be a bundle of laughs tonight. Maybe I'd better read Poe first. Put me in the right mood for writing a humor column.

I sprawled out on the bed with my English book.

For some reason the short story about death, disease, decay, and burial alive did not cheer me up. I closed the book feeling easily as morbid as I had before I'd read the story, only now the shadows on the wall took on a slightly sinister aspect, and the lamp next to my bed — usually adequate for reading the phone book at midnight — seemed to do very little to dispel the murky gloom that had settled into the corners of my room.

The phone rang.

I didn't exactly spring from the bed as if all the devils in hell were chasing me — but I didn't exactly swing my legs gracefully over the side and meander over to answer it, either.

"Hi, Carrie."

Hello yourself, you fink.

"Hello, Claudia."

"Listen, Car, I'm giving a party next week. How about that?"

"How about what?"

"Well, look, it's not like I give a party every week." She sounded indignant that I wasn't screaming for joy.

"What's the matter with you, anyway? You've been acting awfully funny lately."

Funny, I haven't been *feeling* funny lately.

"Are you mad at me or something?"

"Heavens, no, Claudia. Whatever gave you that idea?"

"Carrie, I don't believe you." I can't imagine why not. My voice was positively dripping with sweetness. You could have put a bucket under it and collected maple syrup.

"You *are* mad at me. What did I *do*?"

"Not a thing," I said lightly. "Why in the world should I be angry at you?"

"I'm trying to find that out," Claudia said, exasperated. "Look, I know *something's* wrong. Why don't you just come out with it and stop playing games with me?"

"I wouldn't *dream* of playing games with you," I replied. You might win them. "Am I invited to your party?"

"Well, of course you're invited! That's what I called about! And Marty's coming, and I asked Chip . . ." her voice softened noticeably.

So that was her excuse for hanging around the *Log* office this afternoon! And that must have been the whole reason for the party in the first place! Humph, the oldest gambit in the world. *He'd* never ask her anyplace, so give a party and *she* can legitimately ask *him*.

"I didn't know you knew Chip that well," I remarked, wrapping the curly phone cord around my finger till I nearly cut off the circulation to my nail.

"I don't," she said, "but he was so nice at the football game, and giving me a ride home and all

84

. . ." She let the sentence dangle in midair, fraught with possibilities and implications. Who knew what might happen after the party? Who knew what opportunities the hostess might have for luring the fly into her spiderweb?

"This Saturday or next?" I asked briskly.

"Next. Eight-thirty." She returned brisk for brisk.

"Okay. I'll be there." *Be* there. I wouldn't miss it for the world. If she won, I reserved the masochistic right to be in at my own kill. If she lost, I had an equal right to sadistically rub my hands together in smug satisfaction.

"Well, so long," she said uncertainly.

"'Bye." My voice was cheerful as I hung up.

Well now. Well, well. I leaned back in the chair to think things over.

The phone rang.

"Hey, Carrie."

"Oh, hi, Marty."

"Did Claude call you yet? About the party?"

"Yeah."

"I'll pick you up at eight-thirty, okay?"

"Sure, Marty, sure. That'll be fine."

"How you doing? Anything new?"

You don't know the half of it.

After a few more similarly fascinating examples of how not to make conversation, he hung up.

I needed time to think. If Chip had accepted the invitation to Claudia's party, maybe that meant — no, not necessarily. Chip may have been indifferent to female companionship, but he

85

wasn't a hermit. He went to other parties, had friends. Just because he was going to this particular party was no reason to assume that it was the irresistible attraction of Claudia that —

The phone rang again.

"Grand Central Station," I answered impatiently. The old blue looseleaf sat on my desk, beneath my algebra book. Silent reminders of what I still had to do sometime before tomorrow.

"Carrie?" A muffled whisper.

Oh, no. Just exactly the last thing I needed. A two-hour trip through the emotional wringer with Terry.

"Carrie, I've got to talk to you. Oh, God, it's terrible."

With Terry it was always terrible. There were no grays with Terry — only blacks and whites. And mostly blacks these days. But I'd brushed her off the last time she'd called, and she really hadn't called me since, and I still felt guilty about not having helped her when she wanted help, so I settled back in my chair with a sigh, and said, "All right, Ter, tell Auntie Carrie all about it."

"Oh, Carrie, I know you're sick of hearing it, but I tried calling Claudia, and you know how she just laughs at me, she thinks the whole thing is just a phase, and I'm making a big crisis over nothing; she doesn't know how it feels, Carrie, she's never — I mean, you know yourself you have to *experience* something before you can empathize with a person — "

"Terry," I practically shouted at her, "will you

please *calm down* and try to be coherent? I can't make any sense out of this."

"I'm sorry," she gasped. "I know it's a pain having to listen to this all the time — "

"STOP APOLOGIZING! Tell me what it is, and don't keep saying you're sorry for telling me."

"I just — Carrie, I just can't — " She started to cry, soft little sobs that chopped up her words into nonsense syllables.

"Terry, Terry, it can't be that bad."

"But it *is*. Listen, Carrie." She took a deep breath that I could hear over the phone, and let it come out in a rush. "Carrie, I can't go on like this, I really can't. I know it sounds dramatic, but I can't help it. That's how I feel. I have to do something, I mean, I have to do something *more*. I just can't leave it at that."

"Leave it at what? Terry, what have you done *already*?"

"I wrote a note," she said, her voice barely audible.

"Oh, no, Terry, you didn't!" My heart sank as I tried to imagine the size of the mess Terry had gotten herself into. But it was too big to imagine.

"I didn't sign it," she added hastily. "I made it anonymous."

"But your handwriting," I groaned. "Didn't you realize he could probably figure out who sent it?"

"Maybe I really wanted him to," she admitted hesitantly. It was probably the most perceptive piece of self-awareness Terry had ever revealed.

87

"Well, what happened?"

"Nothing!" she wailed. "Absolutely nothing."

"But Terry," I said, more confused than ever, "what did you *expect* to happen? I mean, what did you hope to accomplish by sending an anonymous note?"

"I don't know," she babbled, "maybe make him interested, kind of stir up his curiosity, or maybe prepare him for something more — "

I couldn't help thinking of the teaser ads that say "Watch this space!" for a week, with a blank box in the newspaper, until finally, your curiosity at a fever pitch, they fill the blank space with the name of a new movie. It was as if Terry were using the very same technique on Mr. Stokes, and it seemed to me frighteningly inappropriate.

"Terry," I began firmly, "you should be very grateful that nothing happened. I think you did a really stupid thing."

"But, Carrie, I tried to ask you — I did, and you practically hung up on me!"

Oh no, I groaned inwardly. Could this possibly have been prevented if I'd listened to her the last time? I wasn't to blame for Terry's stupidity, was I? I'm not responsible —

"All right," I said heavily, feeling much more responsible than I wanted to admit, "all right, Ter, I should have listened to you. But I'm listening now, and I want *you* to listen to *me*. Okay?"

"What?" She sounded ready to go on the defensive at the drop of a hat.

"You must not write any more notes. You must

not approach Mr. Stokes *at all*. I won't tell you to forget him or to channel your thoughts into something constructive. If you want to mope, go ahead and mope. If you want to suffer, go ahead and suffer — "

"But I *don't want* to suffer!"

"All right, just listen. Think about him all you like — dream about him all you like. But don't do *one other* thing about it!"

Silence, except for muffled sobs.

"Terry, did you hear me?"

"Yes, I heard you."

"Terry, please listen. You're going to get yourself into a messy, embarrassing situation if you aren't careful. You may end up getting really hurt."

"But how do you *know*?" she persisted. "Lovey Hart said — "

"Terry, you asked *me*, not Lovey Hart! And besides, like I said last time, she wasn't talking about student-teacher things. She was talking about relationships within our own peer groups." I sounded a lot like my father. I hoped, fervently, that some of his expertise had rubbed off on me.

"But you still don't know unless you try," Terry said.

"Terry" — here I began to sound frantic — "Terry, did you call me to ask my opinion or not? Because if you called to try and convince me to agree with some crazy scheme you have — "

"I can't eat," she groaned, "I can't sleep, I can't concentrate on anything — Carrie, I'm a wreck. You just don't know how I feel, you don't understand . . ." her voice trailed off into a little whimper.

"Terry, give it more time. If you could just wait — "

"I've *given* it time! You think it's just going to cure itself, like chicken pox or something. It's been two months, Carrie, and I still feel the same way. I'll always feel this way, I *know* I will. That's why I have to do something about it."

There was nothing left to say. I couldn't run Terry's life for her, I couldn't force her to listen to me, and short of tying her to a chair for three months, I couldn't prevent her from doing any stupid thing she got it into her mind to do.

Being Lovey Hart was so much easier than being Carrie Wasserman. Once Lovey Hart wrote the definitive answer to a problem there was no back talk, no arguments. Lovey gave her advice, the advisee could take it or leave it, and that was that. Carrie Wasserman gave her advice and all she got was a long explanation of why the advice wouldn't work.

"Well, so long, Carrie. Thanks."

For what? I wondered.

I put the receiver back on the hook and leaned my head on my arms. I wanted to talk this over with Claudia. Claude was sensible, and together we might be able to come up with some way to keep Terry from doing anything rash. After all, Claudia was Terry's friend too.

But hadn't Terry said Claudia just laughed at

her? And how could I talk it over with Claudia when I didn't even feel sure Claudia *was* my friend anymore? Right at the moment, all Claudia seemed to care about was Claudia; she had no time for poor Terry's problems, no worries about hurting my feelings by throwing herself at Chip . . .

The more I thought about Claudia, the angrier I got.

But still . . . I felt kind of empty not being able to talk to her.

TEN

Dear Lovey Hart,
   My mother is an alcoholic. My
father knows it, but can't do anything about it, so he pretends
nothing's wrong. Half the time she's
too drunk to make supper, and I
have to make it. She never cleans or
washes clothes or anything. It's
getting so bad that . . .

Dear Lovey Hart,
   You told me to get this boy's
attention by tickling the back of
his neck in class. Well, I got his
attention and he turned around and
told me to stop fooling with the
back of his neck. But that's all
that happened. What should I do now?

Dear Lovey,
       How can you tell if you're
having a nervous breakdown? I'm
really scared, because I think
there's something wrong with
me . . .

Dear Lovey Hart,
       You told me to talk over with
my parents the situation of not
being able to stay out on dates
past eleven on weekends in a
reasonable way. Well I did, and
they still won't let me stay out
past eleven. What do I do now?

Dear Lovey Hart,
       I am so fat, I hate to look
at myself in a mirror. I've tried
and tried to lose weight, but I
just can't seem to stay on any diet.
Nobody ever asks me out, boys don't
even look at me, and I get so
miserable the only thing that makes
me feel better is eating, and then I
hate myself for not having enough
will power to stop eating . . .

Some people, it seemed, were beginning to talk
back to Lovey Hart. And I didn't now what was
worse — being asked for more help when I hadn't
helped in the first place — or facing the depressing fact that there were some people I couldn't
even try to help. I couldn't answer their letters, so
I didn't use them in the column; they would think
I didn't care because I didn't answer, but what
could I do?

When Marty and I arrived at Claudia's Saturday night, Chip was already there. Claudia greeted us briefly, pointed to where the refreshments were, and then huddled with Chip over a pile of records he was sorting through.

I silently humphed; the old "help me pick out some records" bit was so incredibly unoriginal I felt almost disappointed in Claudia.

"I'm going to get some soda," Marty announced, and walked off to the food table, leaving me staring after him. That certainly wasn't very polite, I thought, and not at all like Marty. Maybe he was in a bad mood because the first-string quarterback (or cornerback) had fully recovered from his injury and Marty hadn't played at all in that afternoon's game.

I caught Chip's eye as he turned away from the stereo.

"Hi," he smiled. Encouraged, I walked over to where he and Claudia stood, instantly dismissing all thought of Marty from my mind.

"Hi, Chip," I said lightly. "Long time no see."

"Yeah. Must be at least twenty-eight hours."

I glanced sideways at Claudia, to see if she was at all bothered by this gentle reminder that Chip and I had far more in common and spent far more time together than she and he ever could. But her face revealed nothing.

"How's the new column coming?" he asked.

"Oh, pretty good. Of course, I'm doing better at thinking up titles for it than thinking up something to *write* in it."

Claudia was now looking at us with barely concealed impatience, as if wondering why, when we had all week to discuss *Log* business, were we talking about that stuff now, when she had more important things on her mind?

"Yeah, well, you've got hardly a week to get something we can put under one of those great titles you're busy thinking up. You better get a move on."

Claudia put a record on the stereo and blasted our conversation with enough decibels to deafen the entire population of Racine, Wisconsin. Subtle.

At that moment, just as Chip's wince of pain made me sure he was going to ask Claudia to turn the damn thing down because we couldn't hear ourselves talk, Marty clamped a hand on my shoulder and said, "Come on and dance."

I turned a puzzled face toward his; it was not the most gracious invitation to the dance I'd ever received.

"Not yet, Marty," I demurred, "nobody else —"

"I want to," he said simply, and pulling me by the elbow, he led me out into the middle of the empty floor and started dancing.

"What in the world — " But the look of grim determination on his face stopped me cold. He certainly didn't look as if he were enjoying our dance; as a matter of fact, he looked more as if he were forcing himself to go through with some unpleasant, but required, chore. I couldn't imagine what had gotten into him. He wasn't acting like the Marty *I* knew at all.

By the time the song ended the room had begun to fill up with people, and I was relieved to end the solo performance we had been giving. Dancing is fine, in a crowd, but I'm not crazy about being in the center of one of those circles where everybody watches and claps as the two best dancers go into their act. Especially since I'm not in the Best Dancer class.

Annoyed, I yanked myself away from Marty and went over to get a Coke. Bob Teal had arrived and was helping himself to food.

"Hi, Twinkletoes."

"Hi yourself, Jock." Which is as inappropriate for Bob as Twinkletoes is for me. He *reports* sports, but that's about it.

"What's happening?"

"You know, I haven't the vaguest idea."

Chip wandered over, threading his way through the now crowded room with Claudia hot on his trail. Most of the people there were her friends from Orchestra, Mathletes, and Physics Club, none of which I belonged to, so although I knew most of them at least by sight, I stayed close to Bob and waited for Chip to reach us.

Chip looked relieved to find someone he knew, and greeted us like long-lost friends. Just as he turned to say something to me, I spotted Marty striding purposefully toward us with the same determined look on his face.

Oh no, not now, I thought helplessly.

And I watched, shocked, as he walked right past me, grabbed Claude by the arm and said, "Come on, Claude, dance with me."

Claudia was just as shocked as I was. She threw me a stunned glance as Marty propelled her to the center of the floor. She had enough time for one lingering, disappointed gaze in Chip's direction before Marty's rather large shoulders blocked her view of us.

I smiled encouragingly at Chip, who was stuffing himself with pretzel sticks almost, it seemed, as if he didn't know what else to do.

You could ask me to dance, I thought, trying to project the idea by telepathy. That would be a nice thing to do, wouldn't it?

"Good food," he grinned sheepishly, as if to explain his sudden gluttony. I didn't consider potato chips, pretzels, and onion dip gourmet fare myself, but I certainly wasn't going to mention that.

"How about," suggested Bob, "a record review column? I thought we could call it 'Logarhythms.'"

"Tsk tsk," I said, "all you ever think of is business."

"That's a great title," Chip commented. "Can you do a column to go with it?"

"Me?" Bob laughed.

"That's the trouble with you people," Chip grumbled. "All you can think up are catchy titles. Nobody seems to be able to get any further than that."

"You can't have everything," Bob shrugged. He put his arm around my shoulders. "Come, my dear," he said, in what was supposed to be a sexy, foreign-movie-idol voice, "I will show you I am not always thinking of business."

My thoughtwaves had richocheted, I surmised, as Bob led me away from the table to dance. Have to be more careful about that from now on.

By this time, thank goodness, more people were dancing, though most were not, so Bob, an enthusiastic but mediocre dancer, and I did not stand out. Or at least not until he got a sudden urge to do an incredibly inept tango which had no relation to the record being played. The results were that we, and several people around us, were reduced to hysterics and I suddenly realized that I was in the spotlight again, this time as comic relief.

"Rudolph Valentino lives!" he cried, spinning me around and lowering me in a death-defying backward dip that had my knees bent and my back parallel to the floor.

"Drop me and I'll kill you," I hissed, feeling that his bent arm was the only thing — and a flimsy-feeling thing at that — keeping me from sprawling on the floor in total mortification.

He lifted me back up again and said in an injured voice, "You have no confidence in me."

Mercifully the record stopped.

And here was Marty again. The minute Bob let go of me, Marty claimed me with a possessive arm around my waist, leaving Bob, to whom he had not said a word, alone in the middle of the floor.

"What was *that* supposed to be?" he asked.

"I think it was *supposed* to be a tango." My voice was cold. I was getting a little tired of being appropriated by him, like private land seized for public use.

"Looked more like Dracula ready to pounce," he muttered irritably.

What had come over him I couldn't begin to imagine. He was surly instead of cheerful, domineering instead of compliant and, in short, so unlike the Marty I knew that I suspected he must have discovered the same formula Dr. Jekyll had imbibed, and had taken several healthy swigs of it before the party.

It couldn't just be the fact that he hadn't played that afternoon, because he didn't play most of the time, and it had never turned him into a sullen boor before.

He pulled me over to a couch and we sat down next to two friends of Claudia's from the Physics Club, Freddie Levine and Myra Connelly. Freddie and Myra immediately launched into a discussion of the game that started Marty off, and I took the opportunity to look around and try and spot Chip.

"Hey," Marty said, shaking my elbow, "I asked you to get me something to drink."

I turned slowly toward him as if not believing what I had heard. I started to open my mouth to say something that would give him a slight indication of what I thought he could do if he wanted something to drink, but I thought better of it. First of all, I didn't want to make a scene; I hate scenes. Second of all, at least getting up to get Marty his Coke would free me from his suddenly constricting clutches for a little while.

"Yes, your highness," I complied, rising to my feet. Myra shot me a look of pure scorn as I did so, and I tried to comfort myself with the thought that she would understand and sympathize if I could only explain the situation to her, but there was nothing I could do at the moment to convince her that I hadn't dealt a deathblow to the Equal Rights movement.

Bob and Chip were standing next to the refreshments just as if they'd never moved from the spot.

"Do you own this concession?" I reached for a paper cup. Where was Claudia? If Chip was alone here without her at his elbow, it was certainly none of her doing.

"I'm not much of a dancer," Chip admitted, as if that explained everything.

"You ought to get Bob to teach you," I grinned.

"I get this definite impression of sarcasm when you say that," Bob frowned.

He looked down at the paper cup I was still holding.

"Aren't you going to drink that?" he asked. "Or are you waiting till it changes into wine?"

"Oh," I remembered, "that's for Marty."

"Hey, yeah, what's with him tonight? He's acting so *weird*."

"I really don't know."

"Maybe he took Lovey Hart's advice," Bob joked.

I nearly dropped the cup. Chip shot me a warning look and I carefully set the cup down on the table. Could that be it? Could Marty have written the letter from Everyone's Brother? Could I actually have inspired this abrupt personality change?

I stared unseeing at the middle of the room, my mind racing to make some sense out of what Bob had said. Would I have recognized Marty's handwriting? Well, no, why should I? He never wrote *me* letters. But why would Marty write to Lovey Hart in the first place?

Well, that was fairly obvious. If he *had* written the letter it was because he wasn't satisfied with things the way they were.

But maybe he hadn't written the letter. Maybe he had just identified with the boy who had, and decided to adopt the tactics I'd suggested.

Which still meant that he was dissatisfied with something about us. But, I reminded myself, there wasn't really any "us" anyway. We were just good friends. Pals. Buddies.

Maybe that's what he was dissatisfied with.

Ridiculous.

But a sense of nagging doubt had intruded. No matter how many times I repeated "ridiculous" to myself I wasn't able to get rid of it.

When my eyes refocused Claudia had reappeared and Bob was saying, "I haven't danced with the hostess yet. My mother always told me to be sure and dance with the hostess."

I grinned at her dismay: I couldn't help it. As he steered her away from where she wanted to be, she looked as helpless as a piece of driftwood in the wake of a tidal wave.

I could almost allow myself to feel the slightest bit sorry for her. If the party had indeed been to give Claudia an opportunity to get her claws into Chip, it certainly wasn't working out the way she'd hoped.

Alone together now, Chip looked at me in a way I can only describe as odd. I can't explain it — except that it made me feel sort of self-conscious; I was very aware that he was looking at me, and I thought I detected a note of something different in his gaze. But I hadn't the slightest idea what it was.

Suddenly I felt this terrific urgency to say something, anything, to distract him, to break his concentration and to help myself stop feeling as if I were being X-rayed by a puzzled doctor in search of an elusive diagnosis. I wished that I had the nerve to stare back at him as frankly and as boldly as he was starting at me — who knew what might happen if our eyes met and he suddenly found himself helpless under the spell of my —

". . . God, what's taking you so long?" Marty demanded.

I forgot how confused and concerned I had been about Marty and me just moments before, I forgot to wonder if Marty was Everybody's Brother, I forgot to care about his feelings at all. I even forgot how much I hate to make a scene.

I was filled with a mindless fury that I didn't even understand.

"Get your own damn soda!" I hissed and elbowed past him to rush out of the room.

Shaking with rage — or something — I practically erupted into the kitchen, much to the surprise of Claudia's mother.

"Oh, hi, Carrie," she said mildly. She was wielding a knife and a ruler, slicing up what looked like the biggest hero sandwich in the world into people-sized portions.

"Having a good time?"

"Yes," I said. It was a struggle not to sound as if I were the guest of honor at my own funeral.

Just then Claudia came in, and seeing me leaning against the table, nodded.

"Having a good time?" she asked.

Why was everyone all of a sudden so concerned with my welfare? I wondered bitterly. And Claudia, of all people. How ironic that she didn't realize the more I enjoyed myself, the worse off she'd be, but, I reminded myself, she had nothing to worry about at the moment, anyway, because I was a safe distance from Chip and, in my present state of mind, I was not in any condition to lure him away from the pretzels.

"Have you seen Terry?" she asked.

"What?" I tried to concentrate on what she was saying. "You mean here?"

"Of course here," she said impatiently.

"No. No, I haven't." I was alert enough now to realize that Terry wasn't around. "Did you invite her?"

"Well, of *course* I invited her."

"So why didn't she come?"

Claudia tilted her head slightly toward her mother, just enough to remind me that Terry's secret was a secret.

"She was kind of vague about the whole thing," Claudia said carefully. "She wasn't sure . . ."

"Maybe she couldn't make it." I tried to sound casual, but the sudden realization that Terry had not shown up made me forget that I was angry with just about everyone I knew.

Was Terry home, alone, contemplating heaven knows what? What she crying? Or was she, at that very minute, too busy planning the move that she thought would get Mr. Stokes to declare himself hers forever? Or actually *making* that move?

"Claude, why don't you call her? Find out why she didn't come?"

"Yeah, maybe I will."

And then, with the same gift for hideously bad timing that he had displayed throughout the entire party, Marty burst into the kitchen.

He looked swiftly around from Mrs. Bailey to me to Claudia, and then back to me again.

"I was looking for you," he said, his voice accusing.

"You found me." I didn't sound as pleased about it as he might have hoped.

"Well," Mrs. Bailey said briskly, "I'll just take these sandwiches in now." She loaded her tray with the speed of an assembly-line worker and seemed relieved at being able to make a quick exit.

Marty looked significantly at Claudia.

"Guess I'll go call Terry," she said, grinning broadly at me.

I didn't see anything at all amusing.

I folded my arms across my chest and radiated hostility toward Marty. Either he didn't feel the vibrations, which is hard to believe since I don't think he could have missed them, or he simply chose to ignore the fact that the chip on my shoulder was only slightly smaller than the Rock of Gibraltar.

"Why did you walk out on me like that?"

"Why are you acting like a Nazi storm trooper?"

"All I did was ask you — "

"You didn't ask! You ordered!"

"Well maybe it's about time I stopped asking and started — "

"What's the *matter* with you? Don't you know how absolutely insane you sound? You're acting like a — "

"Look," Claudia's voice cut in nervously, "I

hate to break up this tender little scene, but Carrie, I really have to talk to you."

Marty glared at her in rage. I'd never seen him look that way before and neither had she, because she said weakly, "Just for a second — you can finish screaming at her in a minute."

She pulled me toward the dining room and whispered urgently.

"Terry won't come to the phone. She's in her room and her mother says she won't talk to me. She tried to get her to, but Terry said she didn't feel like talking now."

"But that's ridiculous. Terry always feels like talking. Maybe she just felt she couldn't have a good long cry with you busy with your party."

Claudia shook her head. "No, because her mother didn't even get the chance to tell her it was me. Terry said she didn't want to talk to *anyone*."

There were too many things hurtling madly around in my head for me to think straight. Chip, Claudia, Marty, Terry, alcoholic parents, fat, loveless girls, ineffectual, self-effacing boys, Jen's possible plotting of revenge for some imagined betrayal; they all suddenly tumbled together into one overwhelmingly confused mass of unresolved questions.

I felt so bowled over that my knees weakened and I grabbed at the back of a chair to steady myself under the weight of it all.

"What do you think?" asked Claudia.

I couldn't think at all. I couldn't solve everyone's problems. I couldn't even handle my own. I wished someone else would start thinking instead of me. I couldn't keep on directing people's lives. I couldn't keep on telling people what to do every step of the way. I was tired of trying to be the assistant stage manager for God.

I shook my head helplessly. I didn't trust myself to speak, because whatever animosity I'd nurtured toward Claudia had abruptly disappeared — maybe because I was just too tired to keep it up anymore — and I was afraid I'd blurt out everything I'd been thinking, the way I'd been used to doing with Claudia for years. I was exhausted by secrets — mine and everyone else's — and nothing would have provided sweeter or faster relief than to spill out everything I'd been holding back for so long right then and there.

"Well," Claude frowned, "if she's in her room and talking, I guess she can't be doing anything too drastic. Oh, hey, I'd better get back to my party. I'm not used to this happy hostess bit."

She surveyed the kitchen.

"The coast is clear," she called back over her shoulder. "He's gone. Coming?"

I dragged myself to my feet, slowly becoming aware of the blare of music and the laughter of people who had forgotten their problems for this one evening at least.

I hardly felt festive, but then again, perhaps the best way to try and shed some of the burdens that seemed so heavy was to plunge right back into the midst of mindless, careless gaiety, and forget thinking and sorting and solving completely; sure, have a good time, laugh, eat, dance, fight with Marty, stay friendly with Claudia while trying to get friendlier with Chip, and keep everybody friendly with everybody else . . .

"Yeah, I'm coming."

ELEVEN

Dear Lovey Hart:
My boyfriend and I are always
fighting because I'm really great in
tennis and hoping to became a pro.
He resents all the time I spend on
tennis and thinks it's stupid to
dream of a tennis career.
What do you think?

                              Confused

Dear Confused,
In tennis, "Love" is zero.
Your boyfriend seems to feel that
in love, tennis is zero. If he resents your choice of a career, maybe
you and he are not cut out to be a
matched set.

On the Monday following Claudia's party, two

things didn't happen. Marty didn't drive me to school and Terry didn't come to school at all. Now either of these things might have happened at any other time without my batting an eyelash, but, coming when they did, I was forced to look beneath the surface for explanations. Not only had Marty ignored me during the entire party after our argument, but he had driven me home in complete silence, having only grudgingly offered a ride and practically sulking when I accepted it.

When he passed my locker just before lunch his only greeting was a curt nod, the sort of bare recognition of acquaintance that might be exchanged between opposing parties in a ten-million-dollar lawsuit.

As for Terry, Claudia was positive that she wasn't sick, at least not physically. Claudia had called her three times on Sunday and each time her mother said she refused to come out of her room.

"She's really worried too," Claude said. We set our lunch trays down at our usual table. "You could tell how upset she was. Her voice was all trembly."

"Well something must have happened," I said. "I mean, this isn't just pining away over unrequited love anymore. Maybe you ought to call her again, and just ask why she isn't in school."

"She's not going to talk to me," said Claude. "What's the use?"

"Look, why don't we just go over there after

school today and force her to talk to us? Go up to her room and stay there until she tells us what's going on. It's too easy for her to refuse to talk on the phone, but if we're sitting right there in the room with her she can't very well ignore us forever."

"It's a thought," Claudia nodded.

"It's the only thing to do."

"Yeah. Well, that's settled then. Oh, hey, I forgot to tell you. Would you believe I got asked on two dates already from my party?"

The meatloaf I'd been chewing seemed to stick in my throat like a wad of sandpaper. No matter how hard I swallowed it wouldn't go down. I didn't want to hear that she had managed to interest Chip after all, and I certainly didn't want to picture the two of them holding hands in the movies . . . I reached for my milk carton, and nearly knocked it over.

"Freddie Levine — you know, the drummer — and your friend Bob from the *Log* both asked me out for next Saturday. Isn't that wild?"

The meatloaf slid effortlessly down my throat as if it had never been threatening to choke me at all. I felt a warm surge of good fellowship toward Claudia. I beamed at her.

"You know," she began confidentially, "Freddie and I have an awful lot in common. Did you know he composes sonatas and things? He might dedicate a concerto to me."

"A drum concerto?" I asked in disbelief.

"Well," she said dreamily, "you never know . . ."

Things were moving just a little too fast for me. I felt like I'd missed a very vital connection somewhere, a piece of information that would clear up my confusion about Claudia's sudden about-face; it wasn't only that she was mooning over Freddie as if Chip had never existed, it was that I'd never heard her daydream about *any* boy this way.

"Claude — " I began helplessly.

"I know, I know, isn't it crazy? I don't know what's gotten into me. You know," she lowered her voice, "for a while there, I thought maybe Chip — but then, when Freddie called, I realized that I was just putting all my emotional eggs into the wrong basket. I mean, here I am, like my mother always said, a late bloomer, and I didn't even know — "

I shook my head in total puzzlement. "I don't follow you at all," I groaned.

"Well, see, I thought that Chip, being so hard to get and all, had to be more interesting than all those other *available* guys; I figured he'd be the kind of person I could fall madly in love with."

"I'm speechless," I said weakly. "Your clinical approach to this whole thing just . . . You know, I'm sure there's a flaw in your logic somewhere. How can you — "

"You can't," she replied, with all the wisdom of an aging courtesan. "You can't force these things."

I wasn't sure whether she was talking about forcing herself to fall in love, or forcing someone else to fall in love with *you*.

"When it happens it happens, and you can't *make* it happen."

"How true," I agreed glumly. Was there a lesson in here somewhere for me? Was I wasting time and effort trying to make It happen between Chip and me when all the time I was overlooking true love in my own backyard? (Meaning Marty.) But no, none of that applied anymore, because now the whole situation had abruptly changed and we were all operating under a new set of rules. Marty was not speaking to me, Claudia had left Chip free to fall into my clutches, and nothing was as it had been — except, of course, that I was still wrestling with the problem of Chip, while Chip was apparently not interested in wrestling with me at all.

Terry's mother seemed glad to see us.

"Maybe you can bring her out of it," she said, but without much conviction. "I've never seen her like this before." She pushed her blond hair off her forehead and pressed her fingers over her eyebrows.

"We'll try," Claudia said.

We went down the hall to Terry's room and Claudia knocked on the door. Without waiting for a response she turned the knob and walked in.

Terry was huddled in a corner of her bed, the covers pulled up to her chest. Her long hair looked dull and limp and her eyes were red-rimmed, with purplish lack-of-sleep smudges circling them.

"Go away," she said hoarsely. "I told my mother I didn't want to talk to anyone."

"So don't talk," Claudia said briskly. She sat down on the edge of the bed. "Don't say a thing. We'll just sit here and watch you feel sorry for yourself."

"Claudia! Can't you see she's miserable?"

"How could I not see? Look at her! Her eyes are all bloodshot and her hair is a mess and she's locked herself in here for three days now. Boy, when this girl is miserable the whole world's going to know about it."

Terry hunched over in her bed and started sobbing. She ignored the box of Kleenex at her elbow.

"Terry, what's the matter?" I pleaded. "Just tell us what it is. It can't be *that* bad."

She cried harder and turned her shoulders away from Claudia, as if trying to pretend we weren't there at all.

I glared at Claudia; it was her fault that Terry had broken down. We weren't going to help her this way at all. But Claude waved away my look. "Leave her alone," she mouthed. "Let her cry."

We let her cry. Her sobs built to a crescendo, then became hiccupy and ragged; her harsh gasps tore at me like claws. I felt her misery and felt helpless in the face of it.

When she finally stopped I was left almost as drained and weak as if I'd been doing the crying myself.

"Now," said Claudia, in a calm, firm tone of voice, "what the hell is the matter?"

And at last, it all came out.

"I went to see him," Terry whispered. "Friday night. I went to his apartment."

I really wasn't very surprised. All along I think I knew this was bound to happen. It was as inevitable as a Greek tragedy. Claudia didn't seem terribly shocked either.

"What happened?" she asked.

"He didn't even let me in. I just stood there, in the hall, and he said I should go home, I shouldn't try to talk to him again — I mean, he knew why I was there before I even told him; and he was so cold — "

She started crying again, but less wildly now, as if she were still too weak to work herself up all over again.

Claudia thrust the box of Kleenex at her and waited.

"And then this woman came to the door behind him, and he said, 'This is Joan, we're going to be married this summer.' And she just stood there practically laughing in my face. And then he said, 'Please go home,' and closed the door on me. And she *laughed*. I could hear her laughing at me right through the door. She thought it was a *riot*."

Claudia handed her another tissue.

"So why didn't you come to school today?" she asked.

"How could I?" Terry wailed. "I can't face him. I made a *fool* of myself!"

"Okay, you made a fool of yourself. So?"

"I can't just walk into his class like nothing happened!"

"Why not? That's what *he's* going to do."

"But I *can't!* He knows now. He'll —"

"He'll what?" Claudia demanded. "He'll treat you exactly the same way he always treated you; no one else will ever know that anything happened. You can't hide out in here for the rest of your life, just on the off chance that you might run into him someday. And that's what you're doing, you know. You're staying out of school because you're afraid to see him in class. *Sure* it'll be hard the first time. You'll feel uncomfortable. But if you do it, then you can do it the second time without feeling so bad. If you don't do it, it'll get harder and harder the longer you wait. And how long do you think you can pull this, anyhow? Your mother isn't going to be sympathetic forever, you know. In a couple of days she's going to come storming in here, throw you out of bed, and either take you to a shrink or send you to school."

Terry just sniffled.

"You don't know how it feels," she said finally.

"Maybe not, but you don't have to be burned at the stake before you can sympathize with Joan of Arc, either. Look, we *know* you feel terrible, we *know* this is the worst thing that ever happened to you, as far as you're concerned. And maybe you're right. But now you've got to say to yourself: Okay, it was terrible, but it happened and I can't go back and do it over, so now I'm going to go on living like it didn't happen."

"Oh, that's so easy to *say*," Terry moaned.

"Well, of course it is. And when something terrible happens to me, I expect you to come and give me the same advice, because I'll probably be too hysterical to think of it myself then. Just like you're too hysterical to see things rationally now."

"And you really think I'll get over it?" Terry asked hopefully. "I mean, you think after the first day it won't be so bad?"

"Now that this happened, I bet you'll get over everything a lot faster than you think. It was like a crisis, you know, instead of a wasting disease, where you just slowly get worse and worse, with no dramatic progress or relapse or anything. This way, you had your crisis, and now you have your terrific, sudden change for the better. You'll see."

She sounded so sure of herself, and so convinced that she was right, that you could practically see the seeds of recovery taking root in Terry's mind.

"I'll call for you tomorrow morning," Claudia said. "You know, give you moral support for your first day."

Terry nodded. She pushed the covers back and hauled herself out of bed.

"Listen, I'm not chasing you or anything, but I really better wash my hair. I'm a mess, huh? You know how long it takes to dry. You can stay if you want — "

"No, that's okay," Claudia said. "I have piles of studying. And Fred might call."

"Fred?"

"Oh, wait'll you hear about my party," Claudia crowed. "And Freddie. Listen, I'll call you later and tell you all about it, okay?"

"Yeah, call me. I'm dying of curiosity." But she was already fumbling through her dresser drawers, collecting odd rollers and absently picking hair out of her round brush. Her mind was obviously only half on what Claudia was saying.

As we went out, Terry's mother stopped us with an anxious look.

"Your daughter will live," Claudia said grandly.

"Claudia, really!" I scolded. "Dr. Freud here," I gestured at Claude, "gave her a good talking-to, and for some reason which I'll never understand, it worked. She really does seem to have snapped out of it."

Mrs. Pasco smiled. "That's good news. But what was it? Did she tell you?"

Claudia hesitated. "Nothing serious — I mean, you know how something which *seems* serious just has to be looked at objectively sometimes, and then you realize it wasn't so serious after all."

Mrs. Pasco looked puzzled.

"She's not too good at explaining things," I said, "but she's a great bargain-basement psychiatrist."

Claudia shrugged. "I'm no Lovey Hart," she

said modestly, "but I do my best with my limited resources."

"Oh, it was awful!" Terry gasped at lunch the next day. "It was terrible, Carrie — I just know he was thinking hideous things about me . . ." She took a hearty bite of her roast beef sandwich and rolled her eyes dramatically.

I tried not to smile.

"Oh, hi, Marty!" she called, as he walked by our table. She looked around eagerly, as if hungry to catch up on what she might have missed after weeks and weeks of moping, trancelike, through lunch.

"Where's Freddie?" she stage-whispered. "Does he have lunch this period? Do I know him?"

Claudia smiled at me, with a smug, self-satisfied look on her face. She should have had a pointy little beard to stroke knowingly while she spouted obscure psychological jargon.

And maybe, I reflected, she would have made a far, far better Lovey Hart than I had ever been.

TWELVE

It had gotten to the point where the sight of that blue notebook in my locker gave me a sinking feeling in the pit of my stomach. I dreaded seeing it there and dredged it up from the general debris with the greatest reluctance. I took it home, stuck it in a drawer, and had fantasies that it would have disappeared the next time I looked for it.

All of a sudden everyone had a complaint. If they didn't find their lives dramatically changed for the better after having followed my advice, they either blamed me for crummy advice, or wanted to know what they should do *now* to fill their lives with thrills and romance. It seemed crazy to write to someone who didn't give you the right answer the first time to get more answers. And I was sick and tired of trying to figure out things for people that they should have been figuring out for themselves.

I was not yet hardened, either, to those letters that posed problems so far beyond my scope that they made me realize just how inadequate I was for this job. I put them to one side and tried to ignore them, but I never really could.

And, oh, how worn out I was from trying to find new gimmicks for the Eternal Number One question: "How do I get him to notice me?"

I began turning from sensible, cute suggestions, to downright sarcastic answers.

"Drop an anvil on his foot."

"Put Jell-O down his shirt."

"Fall off his roof."

At least no one would take me so seriously and maybe, when they realized I couldn't give them any constructive advice, they'd stop writing.

It was kind of Machiavellian, I admit, and it also revealed a vicious streak in me that I didn't know I had. But what else could I do? I begged Chip to drop the column, to let me off the hook, and he absolutely refused to listen.

"It's still the most popular column in the *Log*," he said flatly, "and you're doing a great job. I wouldn't do too much more of that anvil stuff, though. Aw, come on, Carrie, there are only four more issues to go. You can hang in there that long, can't you?"

Could I let Chip the Perfectionist down? Could

I insist on dropping everyone's favorite feature, thus ruining Chip's quest for the Best Newspaper Any High School Had Ever Done? About as easily as I could juggle six plates.

In the meantime I still felt obligated to read every single letter. It was really masochistic. I hardly even tried to answer any of the heavy stuff now, but I felt duty bound to read it anyway — why, I don't know.

And my father, who praised me hugely for my new humor column (which was well received, but stirred up nothing like the interest Lovey Hart did) got more and more irritated on the subject of my alter ego.

"This is tripe," he said disgustedly, "absolute tripe."

I felt a flush of indignation. I wanted to defend myself against his insult; it was all I could do to keep from giving everything away when he attacked me, unwittingly, this way. And yet, secretly, somewhere in my heart, I agreed with him, even if not necessarily for the same reasons. He didn't see all the letters I did, and if he thought *this* was tripe —

"Well, I told Chip your opinion," I said, "even though I didn't have to, according to our agreement. But he thinks the column is too popular to kill."

"But is that the only criterion he uses for the paper? Pornography would be popular too, but should he use it?"

122

"I don't think that's a fair comparison," I said hotly.

"Maybe not, but it's the principle of the thing. Sometimes — no, most of the time — popular and worthwhile are not synonymous at all."

"But *everything* doesn't have to be worthwhile," I retorted. "Some things can be just for fun."

"But people don't take this just for fun. They take it practically as gospel. If Lovey Hart says it, do it."

"Oh, come now. No one takes it that seriously. I mean, is any girl really going to put Jell-O down a boy's shirt?"

"When was the last time you looked in on the freshman lunchroom?"

"I'm in it every day," I reminded him. "You really are exaggerating."

"Maybe a little," he admitted, "but just to make my point."

"You've made it over and over, Dad," I complained. "I understand your point, but there's nothing I can do about it under the circumstances. If you want to pull rank, I can't stop you, but I think there have been court cases about censoring high school newspapers where the kids won."

He grunted that I was right and that was where it usually ended.

One evening about two weeks after Terry's recovery, the phone rang. It was a welcome interruption. I dropped my pen on top of the

Lovey Hart letters (which I'd let pile up till they threatened to overflow my desk drawers) and lunged for the phone with a great sigh of relief.

"Carrie?" Terry's hesitant, uncertain little voice.

Uh-oh, not again. She's supposed to be cured. She'd certainly been acting cured. She'd been as gay and lively as a butterfly during the past week, helloing every boy in sight, sporting new clothes, and asking Claudia and me what we thought of her fourteen latest shades of lip gloss.

"Carrie, I had to ask you, because I feel kind of funny and I want to be sure I'm not going to hurt anyone's feelings or anything."

"What's up?" I asked curiously. "Whose feelings?" It didn't sound so serious.

"Well . . . yours, actually."

Mine? Could it be *Chip*? Could she — oh, of course not! She didn't know anything about how I felt toward Chip. That couldn't be it.

"Well, see, Marty asked me to the spring dance . . . and I feel kind of . . . well, you know, funny. I mean, I don't want to step on anybody's toes or anything . . ."

"You're a great dancer," I said lightly. "You'd never step on anyone's toes."

Was that a twinge of jealousy I was feeling and trying to cover up with a joke? But why should I feel any jealousy at all? Marty and I were nothing but friends, and now we weren't even that. He had a perfect right to go out with anyone he wanted; he'd always had that right — even if he hadn't availed himself of it till now.

"You're sure you don't mind?"

"Why should I mind?"

Why *should* I mind? I really was a dog in the manger. I resented Claudia liking Chip, even though I had no claim in him, and here I was beginning to feel awfully strange about Marty showing an interest in Terry when I hadn't even *wanted* him to be interested in me, *ever*.

"Well, that's okay then," Terry said, sounding relieved.

Jen came in and sprawled on my bed.

After a few more desultory exchanges with Terry, I hung up.

"What is it with you," I asked Jen, "and that phone? It's like Pavlovian conditioning — every time the phone rings you head for my room."

"What's Pavlovian conditioning?"

"Never mind, you'll get to it in Biology. What do you want?"

"Oh, I just thought we might talk," Jen said idly.

"Okay. What do you want to talk about?"

Jen examined her fingernails with greatly exaggerated concern for the one or two ragged cuticles there.

"I know something," she said softly, "that you don't know I know."

Bam. There it was. Feeling as if the world were about to cave in on me, I tried not to look over at my desk, where the Lovey Hart letters lay in plain view. I had to hide my dismay, I reminded myself, and not let Jen see that I was worried. Maybe she wouldn't be able to blackmail me if I could manage to convey the impression that I was totally unconcerned about whatever she knew.

"I'll bet you know lots of things," I said lightly.

But she wasn't going to fall for that approach. "Maybe. But I know one thing that you wouldn't want me to tell Daddy."

She lay back on my bed as if she owned the place. She looked so smug and in command of the situation that I was tempted to smack her.

"Well? Are you going to tell me what it is, or are you enjoying yourself too much to reveal your deep, dark secret?"

"I know," she gloated, "who you are."

Any remaining doubt or hope was now effectively shattered. I slumped onto the bed, almost, but not quite, ready to admit defeat. I had to at least try to brazen it out.

"And I know who you are," I said in a bantering tone. "That makes us even."

Jen's eyes narrowed. She was through letting me fool around with her.

"Yeah, but I don't have to hide who I am," she said. "You wouldn't want anyone to know you're Lovey Hart."

The game was now officially over. Time to consolidate my losses, evaluate my position, make a deal with the enemy, and do a lot of heavy praying.

126

"How did you find out?"

"Really, Carrie," she said condescendingly. "You leave those letters all over the place, and with your writing on the bottom of them and all..."

"They weren't 'all over the place,'" I retorted. "They were in my own, private desk drawers. You were going through my things — you were snooping!"

"When Daddy finds out you're Lovey Hart I think he's going to be madder at you than he is at me," she said confidently.

"That's really rotten, Jen! I don't go pawing through your room, invading your privacy. Why do you want to make trouble for me?"

Jen looked uncomfortable for the first time since she'd started this.

"I don't exactly want to make trouble for you," she muttered.

"Well then, what is it? Why are you so mad at me that you want to go tattling like a little kid?"

She hesitated. She seemed almost embarrassed now, as if reluctant to tell me why she had it in for me.

"Well, you remember that pajama party I wanted to go to?"

"Oh, Jen, you're kidding!" That was ages, eons, millennia ago. I couldn't believe it was still on her mind.

"You took *their* side," she said angrily. "You all treated me like I was a dumb little child. Even Marty. You all laughed at me."

127

"But you can't still be mad at me for that! Jen, that was months ago."

"Well, that's what started it. Ever since then you've been chasing me out of your room, hiding things from me, always acting like you had these big important secrets — "

"So you went through my things, looking for something to get revenge with?"

"Well, you and Chip made me suspicious that day you were in here whispering and banging drawers and things. I figured you were hiding *something*."

"So?"

"So when you acted so mean to me all the time I decided to find out what it was. Then it wouldn't be a big secret anymore and you'd stop chasing me away — and everything. And you'd have to be nice to me, because you'd be afraid I'd tell."

"Oh, Jen, what can I say? I'm really sorry I hurt your feelings; I certainly didn't mean to. And if you're convinced you have to pay me back I can't stop you either."

I felt saddened by it all. Not just worried about what would happen after she told, but upset by the idea that she felt I'd so wronged her that she had to hurt me back. Sure, I'd been impatient with her for a while now, and she probably felt that I snapped at her constantly these days; but it had all started with her sneaky, "I'm watching you" attitude that had kept me continually on edge. It isn't easy to be nice to someone who's deliberately trying to make you nervous.

"I don't know," Jen sighed. "This didn't turn out the way I pictured it."

"What do you mean?"

"Well, you're not screaming at me or begging for mercy or bribing me or anything," she said, avoiding my eyes as if she were ashamed of what she was saying. "I sort of thought I'd really enjoy threatening you and all. You know, you're always able to order me around because you're older and I thought this one time, I'd be able to order *you* around because . . . well, you know."

"I didn't know you felt that way. I'm sorry if you think I've been bossy."

I *was* sorry, but I didn't really think I'd been all that bossy. But what difference did the actual truth make compared to what Jen *felt* was the truth?

"You know, it just doesn't seem to matter much anymore," Jen said dully. "I don't even care. It *was* a long time ago. And they didn't even have the pajama party anyway."

"What?"

"Yeah. Alice's mother wouldn't let her. She said it was all girls or nothing, so they didn't even have it."

Now Jen really looked uncomfortable. The whole thing had been so pointless, so childish — and yet, I really must have insulted her for her to have carried it so far . . .

"You know what, Jen?" I asked suddenly.

"What?"

"I still love you."

She looked up at me, surprised, and slowly her face brightened.

I glared at the pile of Lovey Hart letters on my desk. I really ought to get on with the damn things, I thought. Then I looked back at Jen, smiling openly at me for the first time in weeks. Sometimes, I told myself firmly, you have to get your priorities in order.

"Hey, how would you like a manicure?" I took one of her hands and examined it. "You have very good nails, you know? We could use that new stuff I got, it's really nice — Glacéed Peach, I think it's called."

"Would you?" she said. Then she scowled. "Oh, no, Mom wouldn't let me wear nail polish."

"Oh, sure she will. It's very pale. Once she sees how nice your hands look, she'll let you keep it on."

"I'm sorry I went through your drawers," Jen said softly.

"I know you are," I replied. I reached down to give her a hug and she clutched at me for a second, and then let go.

"Come on," I said with a big grin, "let's go find that manicure kit."

THIRTEEN

Dear Lovey Hart:
     I wrote to you about my mother
being an alcoholic and you never
answered me. All you write about
mostly are silly unimportant problems, but when it comes to something
practically life or death, you cop
out. You're supposed to be there to
help, and I really needed help, but
I guess I wasn't important enough
to get your attention, or maybe you
just use these letters as excuses to
make your snide remarks, and don't
even care about the people who write
to you . . .

Dear Lovey Hart:
     I wrote to you a couple of
months ago about being fat and you
told me to diet and I did because
you convinced me that I would be

miserable as long as I went on the
way I was going. So I went on a diet
of nothing but bananas and grape-
fruit and nearly ended up dead of
malnutrition. I was so out of it I
had to see the doctor, and he said
it was very irresponsible of you to
tell me to go on a diet without
checking with my doctor first . . .

Dear Lovey Hart:
      You are a fraud. I don't know
where you got the idea you could
help people, but let me tell you how
you "helped" me . . .

I am convinced that bad things, like grapes,
come in bunches. When everything is blackest,
you can be sure there's more where that came
from.

Lovey Hart had changed from savior to scape-
goat.

The trickle of dissatisfied letters slowly in-
creased until a good half of all the letters ad-
dressed to Lovey complained either about the
advice I'd given or that I hadn't given any advice
at all.

What do you think I am, I wondered, some
kind of guru? How do they expect me to answer
one hundred and fifty letters in a column that
only runs to about eight column inches?

Well, of course the thing was, they *did* think
I was some sort of guru — that's just what I'd
been advertised as. And it never entered their
minds that anyone else's problem was as earth-

shaking as theirs. So if I didn't use someone's letter in the column, it was because I didn't care. And if I did answer someone's question, and his or her life didn't suddenly turn into a rose garden, it was *my* fault. After all, wasn't I the one who told them what to do? And if they took my advice, and followed it to the letter, how could they be blamed if everything didn't turn out happily ever after?

As it had once been the fad to read every word Lovey Hart wrote, it was now fashionable to criticize every answer, to quote, with hoots of derision, from my latest words of wisdom.

I don't know how it started, or why it mushroomed the way it did, but it was as if all the malcontents got together, compared notes, and decided to spread the word that Lovey Hart was a blockhead. To be honest, my attitude toward the column was probably partly responsible for the change. Because it was when I got fed up and started writing all those crazy things about dropping anvils on people and slipping Jell-O down boys' shirts that they got fed up with Lovey Hart.

Whatever the cause, it was bad news, and although Chip kept urging me to ignore the growing rumbles of displeasure, it was harder and harder to hear people attacking Lovey (who was *me*, after all) without feeling personally hurt and insulted.

"But you're still selling papers," Chip never tired of pointing out. "They're still reading you just as much as ever."

"That's fine for you to say," I retorted. "You're not the one they're threatening to lynch.'

Chip kept trying to calm me down, but by this point I was beyond calming. I was running to him on the average of three times a week, begging for mercy; all thoughts of pleasing him were wiped out of my mind, my fantasies about being perfect enough to sweep him off his feet were forgotten. All I dreamed of now was getting out from under the deluge of letters and sneers that threatened to drown me.

Yet every once in a while, when I spoke to Chip, I got a fleeting impression of being stared at again the way I thought he'd been looking at me at Claudia's party. It was a funny kind of a stare, nothing you could exactly put your finger on, but maybe the way you look at someone when you're trying to assess how you feel about them. I don't know and I didn't really pay that much attention to it then anyway, because to me the main thing was to trade in my Lovey Hart suit for my old Carrie Wasserman clothes, and nothing could have distracted me from that effort.

But I did get those fleeting impressions.

Despite Chip's determination to keep Lovey Hart, I began to work on my last Lovey Hart column during spring vacation. I was just as determined to quit as he was to keep me on, and the barrage of critical, complaining, attacking letters I brought home with me over the vacation served to bring my desperation to the breaking point. If I'd needed to convince myself any further that I was not cut out for the advice game, that batch of letters did the trick.

The last column would have no letters, no advice, just an explanation of why Lovey Hart was going to disappear in a puff of smoke, never to be heard from again. Once Chip read this, I was sure he would finally understand that I meant business.

But it turned out to be a harder column to write than I'd thought. I couldn't get the right tone to it, and no matter how much I tried to write, rewrite, and change words around, it kept coming out sounding sulky and vindictive. Maybe that was because I *felt* sulky and vindictive, but it just wouldn't do to let Lovey Hart go out in a blaze of nastiness.

Vacation ended, school started again, and the column still wasn't written. The *Log* deadline was barely a week away and my wastepaper basket was filled with the crumpled remnants of my struggle.

On Saturday the senior class held its annual Spring Carnival and I volunteered to take Jen. That isn't as altruistic as it sounds. I didn't have anyone to go with except Jen. Claudia was going with Fred and Terry was going with Marty. They both asked me to come along with them, but naturally I didn't like the idea of being the old fifth wheel any more than I wanted to go by myself, so I was left with my sister.

Jen insisted on getting there at 10 A.M., when the thing started, and surprisingly enough there were already plenty of people milling around the school grounds when we arrived. It was a gorgeous day, warm and sunny and cloudless; music blared over the PA system, seniors, some with bullhorns, bellowed out spiels for their various games and booths, and the noise and sunshine and gaiety of the whole atmosphere combined to drive away just about all of the self-pity I'd been indulging in.

"Carrie, let's get some cotton candy," Jen said eagerly, "and then walk around and see what we want to do."

"It's too early for cotton candy," I protested. "I've hardly woken up yet."

"Oh, come on. Anyway, they haven't got all the games set up so we might as well start eating."

"Jen, you never need an excuse to eat."

I followed her to the cotton candy booth. As she paid for it, I looked around for someone I knew.

"Want some?" Jen held out the paper cone.

"No thanks. That stuff is death on teeth."

"Oh, Carrie, once in a while it won't kill you."

Although the place was rapidly filling up with kids, not all of the games and things were ready yet and Jen, who is sort of a connoisseur of carnivals, was dividing her time equally between playing the games that were already set up and trying to guess what the uncompleted booths were going to be.

And, being physically unable to pass anyone selling anything for human consumption without partaking, she was also doing a great deal of eating.

Within an hour Jen had bought — in addition to the cotton candy — a hot dog, Italian ices, and a bag of potato chips. She had also won a goldfish by tossing a Ping-Pong ball into his bowl. Whenever Jen ate something, I had to carry the goldfish — and that was a good part of the time since what she was doing most of was eating — and reassure her that I *was* being careful, and no, I wouldn't drop George.

"George is probably the only pet in the entire world that I'm not allergic to," Jen kept reminding me.

"Hey, Carrie!" I turned around to see Terry hurrying toward us, pulling a reluctant-looking Marty by the hand.

"Hi, Jen," Terry said, catching up with us.

"Hi!" Jen looked uncertainly at Marty, then frowned at me, as if wondering about the situation.

"Hi, Jen," Marty mumbled.

"Hi," she said coolly.

"Where'd you get the fish?" Terry asked.

"Over there." Jen pointed. "I threw a Ping-Pong ball into his bowl. His name is George. It's easy. You could win one."

"Oh, yeah, look, Marty, it's only a quarter. Hey, that's pretty good. Even if the fish died, the bowl would make a really neat planter."

Jen looked aghast. If she could have, she would have covered George's ears, so he wouldn't be upset by such talk. She gazed down at him and murmured something comforting.

Terry was already heading for the goldfish booth. Marty started to follow her, then suddenly turned around and looked at me, his eyes searching my face.

"Carrie, I — " He groped helplessly for words. He glanced at Jen, who made a very theatrical display of looking the other way, as if she were totally disinterested in anything he had to say to me.

"I'm sorry," he said finally. "I acted like an idiot."

"I'm sorry too."

"It was that Lovey Hart," he blurted. "That stupid column about not being such a nice guy. I thought — well, you know, you were taking me for granted."

Although Jen had her head turned the other way, I could see her body was absolutely rigid — I don't think she was even breathing, so intent was she on not missing a word of the conversation she was pretending not to hear.

"But that was what was nice," I said sadly. "Taking each other for granted. Being *friends*."

"Yeah, I guess so. But I think I got to a point where I wanted — I mean — " He struggled to find a way to say it. He pulled me a little distance away from Jen and lowered his voice.

"Carrie, I thought we ought to — be different

138

with each other, you know what I mean? So I tried to — " He sighed and shrugged.

I knew exactly what he meant, and knowing it was making me feel awfully uncomfortable.

"But that wasn't right for us," I said uneasily. "And now you have someone — well, why can't we just go back to being friends again?"

He looked enormously relieved.

"Well, sure, that's what I want," he said happily. "Just like it was before."

"Right," I nodded. "Just like it was before."

But it wouldn't be, of course. Lovey Hart, in her own inimitable fashion, had seen to that. Marty and I would be talking to each other again, but that was about all that would remain of what we'd been. He would be at Terry's beck and call, driving Terry to school and home again, meeting Terry for pizza after football games. Sure, they'd ask me to go along sometimes, but nothing would be the same anymore.

I felt as if one whole chapter of my life had come to an end, and it made me sad. No, I never entertained any romantic thoughts about Marty, but it had been a comfortable sort of thing, a relationship I took for granted as part of my life. It was true, what he'd said. I *had* taken him for granted, and even if he didn't agree, I thought that was as nice in its own way as grand passion was in *its* way. Not as exciting, of course, not as emotionally fulfilling, not even worth writing in your diary about — but *nice*.

Terry came running back.

"Marty, would you try? I couldn't do it. It *looks* so easy."

Jen turned her head back toward us and looked disgusted.

"It *is* easy," she muttered.

"Well, we'll see you around later," I said. "Good luck with your fish."

Terry took Marty's arm and led him away.

Jen, who was now impatient to get moving again said, "Come *on*, Carrie," and started working her way through the crowd to find a booth where there weren't too many people waiting to play.

Would it have happened this way if I'd never written the Lovey Hart column, I wondered? Or would it just have been a matter of time before Marty decided on his own that he wanted to be "more than a brother" to someone and that someone wasn't me?

I followed Jen through the crowd, picking my way carefully around shrieking kids who didn't seem to care when their ice cream and cotton candy came into contact with your clothes. I shielded George from harm as I elbowed my way through the mob. The water in his bowl was getting choppy, but at least I was going to make sure that no careless kid waving his food around was going to condemn George to death by pizza.

Jen won a straw hat with "Lincoln Senior Class" on the band by knocking down three milk bottles with a baseball. She put it on proudly, and without even a pause to savor her triumph headed for the nearest refreshment stand.

"Think George would like a piece of hamburger roll?" she asked between bites.

"No," I said firmly. "I'm sure he wouldn't."

"Boy, all this fresh air gives me an appetite."

"*Everything* gives you an appetite."

She polished off her hamburger and Coke and tossed the cup and napkin into a trashbasket.

"I'll hold George for a while," she said. "I want him to get to know me."

She took the bowl from my hands and bent her head to talk to her fish. I wriggled my fingers, which felt stiff from carrying the bowl around all morning, and began to feel my good mood slip away, to be replaced by the self-pity I'd started out with.

Everyone was with someone, friends, boy friends, the little kids with parents fussing over them, wiping their faces, doling out quarters and generally caring whether or not they were having a good time. The amplified music, which had seemed festive an hour ago, now crashed about my head, pounding into my brain and giving me about as much pleasure as being caught in the crossfire between rival street gangs.

The seniors running the booths and shouting in carnival barker style no longer seemed funny or fun. They were secure in their straw hats, they had status and they belonged; they were a part of something that I felt very left out of, and their security made them seem smug, self-satisfied, and show-offy. They looked every bit as in control of their destinies as they were of their little corners of the carnival; I was sure they ran both with equal efficiency and confidence.

How I envied them at that moment. I had let almost everything I'd been involved with get out of control and I felt as helpless at running my own life as I'd been as Lovey Hart, trying to run other people's lives.

"BOO!"

I jerked my head around. Bob Teal and Chip were standing right behind me.

"You scared me," I said, trying to sound annoyed, and failing. I was delighted to see them. My spirits zoomed back up again; I had friends, I belonged, the rest of the day would be lovely.

"Chip, you know Jen," I said. "And Jen, this is Bob Teal."

"Hi," said Bob.

"And this is George," Jen introduced her fish.

"Pleased to meet you," Bob said solemnly into the bowl. "Does he shake fins?"

Jen giggled. "No, I haven't taught him that yet. I just won him."

"Well, he looks pretty intelligent," said Bob. "I wouldn't be surprised if he were shaking fins in no time."

"Been here long?" Chip asked me.

"Oh, about an hour. They did a really good job, didn't they?"

He nodded. He was looking at me in that strange way again. What was he *thinking*? I wondered, wishing I could open his mind like a book, and read what was happening in there.

Funny though. This time I didn't feel uncomfortable or self-conscious, despite the intensity of his gaze. It was almost . . . exhilarating, like a challenge. He must, I realized, be looking at me this way because he finds me interesting, even fascinating! Why else isn't he able to take his eyes off me? I remembered the many times during the past week when he'd looked at me the same way and I'd shrugged it off. Now it all seemed to add up.

And suddenly I *felt* like a fascinating person. After all, I must be, I reasoned, if Chip thinks so.

I began to glow, like a small sun. I smiled, confident that my smile was dazzling enough to warm everyone in my little corner of the universe. Chip smiled back. Together we could light up the world.

"Chip," I said later, as we watched Jen and Bob try to score twenty-one on a Blackjack Toss game, "remember that day at my house when you were so upset about the *Log*?"

"And you told me I was a perfectionist? Sure, I remember."

"Why did you feel that way?"

He grinned and tried to sound mysterious. "If I tell you, then you'll know what makes me tick."

"Don't you want me to know? I mean, is it a deep, dark, ugly secret?"

"Let's put it this way," he said. "If you know everything about a person right away, what's there to look forward to?"

My stomach gave a funny little jump. He had practically come right out and said that we would be getting to know each other better. He was projecting a future for us. It's one thing to feel in your bones that someone you care about cares about *you*; it's another thing entirely to hear him practically announce it.

My fingers began to tremble so hard that George, whose bowl I was holding again, could have taken up surfing if he felt like it.

I stared down at the bowl and tried to will my hands to stop shaking.

"Carrie, look! Bob won!"

Jen dangled a string of red beads in front of my face.

"He rolled a twenty-one, and he got this for me!"

She beamed at Bob with the same look of devotion she had formerly reserved only for Marty.

"Oh, it was nothing," Bob said with mock modesty.

"It was *too* something," Jen insisted. "*I* couldn't do it."

"Well," Bob laughed, glancing at Jen's pockets stuffed with things she'd already won, "then it was the only thing you *couldn't* do as far as I can tell."

"Oh, Carrie, look," Jen said, pointing down toward the parking field, where there were more booths set up. "Let's go over that way. They're just opening now; it's not so crowded."

We followed Jen as she darted through the mob.

"Kid would make a great broken field runner," Bob remarked. "She thinking of taking up football?"

"Not that I know of," I laughed, "but with Jen you never can tell."

As we got closer to the booths, Jen yelled back, "Hey, Claudia and Terry are there." She waited for us to catch up. "I'll take George now. I want to show him to Claudia."

She took the bowl carefully from me and said, "There are some people I want you to meet, George."

"Uh, isn't she a little hysterical about that fish?" Bob asked uncertainly.

"Well, she's allergic to everything else," I explained. "She's never really had a pet."

"Hey, Carrie!" Claudia shouted and waved as she saw us approaching. Fred was standing next to her, his arm draped comfortably over her shoulders.

I started to wave back, then dropped my arm and grabbed Chip's wrist.

"Look!" I hissed, clutching at him frantically.

The booth that Jen was leading us to had a big sign on the front which read LET LOVEY HAVE IT! Seated underneath a bucket of water was a boy dressed in a flowered tent dress with a string mop on his head, lots of red lipstick, and big, black-framed glasses. They were throwing baseballs at

145

the bucket trying to overturn it and soak "Lovey Hart."

I felt sick.

It was *me* that they wanted to drench, me that they were drowning in effigy; all that anger and hostility that had been building up against Lovey Hart was masquerading here as "fun" and it was all directed at *me*.

I hung back, not wanting to see any more, not wanting to go over there and watch as Marty threw baseballs at my stand-in. It was an awful feeling and all I wanted was to get out of that place, go home, and stop being Lovey Hart.

Chip whispered, "Hey, take it easy," and uncurled my fingers from around his wrist.

"But it's *me*," I whispered back. Jen was walking very slowly, carefully watching George's bowl as she carried him over to meet Claudia. "Don't you see why I can't — "

"Now don't go schizo on me," Chip murmured, taking my hand. "It's not you, it's just a symbol. Lovey Hart is a noted school personality, that's all."

Pulling gently at my hand, he led me forward.

And then Jen, who had been more concerned with transporting George safely than with where she was heading, looked up and saw the sign on the booth.

"Carrie!" she shrieked, in a voice that could have drowned out a formation of Air Force jets thundering overhead. "Carrie, they've got a whole booth about you!"

FOURTEEN

It took a moment for the stricken look to cross Jen's face. It took a moment for the small group gathered in front of the booth to make the connection and then to turn their heads, practically in choreographed precision, toward me. I was horribly frozen to the spot where I stood, watching what looked like a slow-motion film clip, as bewilderment gradually changed to recognition, then to various expressions of outrage, shock, or glee on the faces that confronted me.

The boy dressed as Lovey Hart bounded off his stool and raced over to me, clutching the sides of his dress. He grabbed my arm and pulled me toward the booth.

"I've been saving your seat for you," he said wickedly.

I yanked my arm free. I felt the beginning of panic and looked wildly to Chip for help. His face was as shocked as mine must have been and he looked equally helpless.

Terry and Claude started toward us and Jen, clasping George's bowl against her stomach, was in tears.

"So you're Lovey Hart," said the boy who was standing in front of the booth. "This is terrific!"

He picked up his bullhorn and put it to his lips.

"Ladeez and gentlemen! Your attention please!"

"No!" I screamed. "Don't!"

People were now clustered around me, not only Claude and Terry, but others, grabbing my arm to get my attention, shouting to be heard, all talking at once. I couldn't understand what they were saying, I was too confused to read the expressions on their faces or to sort out their voices; all I could think of was that I was in the middle of an ugly mob. Whether that was true or not, I didn't know — all I knew was that I felt terrified and wanted desperately to get away from them all.

Chip and Bob both had their hands on the bullhorn and were urgently conferring with the boy who was about to use it.

Apparently they were successful, because I didn't hear him blare out my name, but I didn't wait around to find out for sure.

I plowed through the people who surrounded

148

me, wildly shoving arms out of my way, and ran toward the parking lot.

I didn't look back.

Chip came running. I leaned against a car trying to catch my breath and calm myself down.

"I'll take you home," he said. All I could manage was a weak nod.

"How did she know?"

"She found out," I said hoarsely. "I was careless."

"Carrie! Carrie!" Jen cried, walking toward us as fast as she could without spilling George.

"Carrie, I'm sorry!" Tears streamed down her face.

"I know." I felt more sympathy than anger for her. "You didn't mean to do it."

She shook her head helplessly.

"Hey," I tried to joke, "don't cry in George's bowl. I think he's a freshwater fish."

Jen sniffled and tried to smile.

It was more than I could do.

The first few days were terrible. My father hardly spoke to me and took no trouble to disguise the look of disappointment on his face. My parents thought I'd been sneaky and dishonest with them, and while there was no mammoth explosion, this was even worse.

They acted as if I'd betrayed a trust and I didn't even have the comfort of feeling unjustly maligned, because the fact was that I *had* been secretive and I *had* hidden things from them — and had gone on and done the very thing I knew my father heartily disapproved of.

And to make me feel even rottener, they understood, or said they understood, when I tried to explain that I had to make my own decisions and do the things that I thought were important and establish my own values and ideals. They knew all that, they agreed. Hadn't they tried to raise me to be able to do exactly that?

But that didn't mean, they pointed out, that they had to approve of what I did, or agree with my values, any more than I had to agree with theirs. And they couldn't, they emphasized, help being disappointed with me and hurt that I hadn't consulted with them or confided in them.

Claude, Terry, and Marty were hurt, and in very much the same way my parents were.

"You could have told *us*," Terry said indignantly. "We're your best friends. There I was going on and on about what Lovey Hart said, and you never said a word. What an idiot I was!"

Both Terry and Marty felt I had played them for fools; instead of taking advice from plain old Carrie Wasserman, their friend, they had gone to Lovey Hart, the expert, and when it turned out that we were one and the same, it seemed as if they'd never forgive me for tricking them that way.

Not everyone was hostile, though a lot of people made pretty cutting remarks, and it was hard to get through lunch without being constantly interrupted by people who just "had to get this one thing" off their chests. A couple of people actually thanked me in person, one of whom was my ex-drug addict from the very first column I'd written.

When Claudia and Terry heard that one — they were still eating lunch with me for some reason — the recriminations and resentments seemed to ease up a bit and I began to think for the first time that they might actually forgive me.

It died down. Everything does, if you wait long enough.

At the risk of stirring it all up again, Chip printed the last Lovey Hart column, which I finally had managed to write in the midst of that terrible week, in the May issue of the *Log*.

He asked if I was sure I wanted it printed and I said I was. There were some things I had to get off my chest, too.

Dear Readers,
     This is my last column as Lovey Hart.
     I tried to help you. To those of you whom I did help, and who told me so, thank you. To those of you I didn't help -- and there were plenty -- all I can say is, I tried and I'm sorry. To those of you who thought I treated your problems frivolously, I apologize for that too.
     I'm sure I learned a lot more from all of you while I was writing this column than you learned from

me. Like one thing I learned was
maybe I shouldn't have tried to
write this column at all!

I guess it boils down to this:
You can't have easy answers to tough
questions -- maybe you can't have
easy answers to any questions. And
maybe the only person who can solve
your problem is you. In any case,
Lovey Hart (alias Caroline Wasserman) has run out of answers.

I wish everyone love.

"Sure sounds humble," Chip grinned, as he read it over again. We sat perched on desks in the *Log* office with Bob, Terry, Marty, Claudia, and Fred.

Terry folded up the paper.

"I think it sounds preachy," she said.

"Well, preachy *and* humble," Bob suggested.

"Neat trick," remarked Claude. "How'd you manage that?"

"It wasn't easy," I said truthfully. "How do you think people will take it?"

Chip laughed. "Some people will think it's preachy."

"And some," Bob finished, "will think it's humble."

"Well," I sighed, "at least it's *over*."

"You mean," Marty said, "that you're not going to make this your life's work?" It was more good humor than he'd shown me in a long time.

I threw a book at him.

Just then my father stuck his head in the door.

I bit my lip nervously, wondering if he was going to say something about the column, about the whole Lovey Hart affair, in front of all my friends. I wondered if I could even blame him if he did break our agreement, considering . . .

"Just wanted to let you know," he said, with a devilish grin on his face, "that that was the best Lovey Hart column I've ever seen."

"Thanks," I said. I breathed a sigh of relief. The worst was over.

"I still say it was a good column," Chip insisted as my father went off down the hall.

"Was," I reminded him sharply. "The key word is *'was.'* "

"Well, one good thing came of it," Chip murmured. He gave me a frank, affectionate smile that made my toes curl.

"Now what could that be?" Bob wondered. He tapped a forefinger against the side of his nose.

"I can't imagine," I sighed.

About the Author

Ellen Conford was born in New York City and now lives in Massapequa, Long Island, New York with one sheepdog, two cats, one son who is in college and one husband who is a professor of English. She started writing when she was in the third grade but her first book wasn't published until after she was grown up. She has published fifteen books for children of all ages. She is the 1981 champion of Scrabble Club #32, Massapequa, New York.